ACKNOWLEDGEMENTS

People sometimes say that the measure of your success in life can be traced to your parents, in one form or another. For some, the challenge of difficult or missing parents inspires them to drive harder. In my case, two unique parents are the foundation for my communication skills and my desire to include everyone and see them become the best version of themselves. A wise man taught me to "Just Be." Despite difficult circumstances, my father found the courage to be the best version of himself. My mother personifies dignity, grace, truth and love. To both my parents, who gave me my third language, my respect, gratitude and love. Both deaf mutes, they have always been far from silent! I take them with me wherever I go, beginning and ending each of my speeches in their language - one I share with love.

Knowing that I am supported by two remarkable people,

I take their legacy of love and pay it forward.

To my wife Wanda, who believes in me and always has my back. And my daughter April, who puts my life into proper perspective every time I see her. I'd like to thank both "my girls".

To John, who gave me everything he had to start my business. Thanks for being everything a brother could want.

To Jeff, who allowed me to share his journey as an athlete and who shares with me every day as we build the business. Thanks for playing "this game" with me.

To my sister Juanita, who makes sure the "kid" is alive and well in all of us. Thank you for showing us where the magic lives. Like Mom, you have grace and love, and you know how to create a place called "home."

To "my other family", my thanks for your energy, commitment, loyalty and for helping FFG to grow into the best version of itself. Thanks for playing the game of life and running the marathon with me.

And finally, my thanks to all the speakers, consultants and authors worldwide, who have preceded me. Many of you have paved my way and provided me with aspects of what has become a blueprint for my own success. I will do my best to pay forward the gifts you have given me.

PASSION *for* POSSIBILITY

Moving beyond believing ... *INTO KNOWING*

JUST BE

Jose Feliciano, CFP, ChFC, CLU, LUTCF

Passion for Possibility:
10 Keys to Moving beyond believing . . . Into Knowing

Copyright © 2009 by Jose Feliciano

www.felicianofinancial.com

Printed in the United States of America

TABLE OF *Contents*

FROM THE AUTHOR

Success unshared doesn't do much. Paying it forward and sharing the steps along the way is as important as getting "there." I have stood on the shoulders of giants to get where I am today. This book is my steppingstone for those of you who don't want to reinvent the wheel.

If you believe a person can learn from their mistakes, but a smart person learns from other people's mistakes, then I invite you to borrow shamelessly from this book. I would be honored to know that something you read here might just give you an "aha" moment.

I learned that when the student is ready the mentor or teacher appears . . . sometimes even within the pages of a book.

CHAPTER One

ENVISIONING YOUR GOALS FROM FINISH TO START

Driving to the university on the morning of my speech, it was a beautiful spring day and the crepe myrtles in Tyler, Texas, were in full bloom. They were bursting with potential. Just like the students I was about to address. Going over my notes in my head, I considered the speech I was about to deliver.

As a Certified Financial Planner and owner of a Wealth Management firm, addressing a graduating class in finance, I knew I could discuss the intricacies of the financial world that they were so anxious to enter. However, my heart kept prompting me to talk about something else altogether. What could I teach these students that would possibly stick with them more than just another speech about financial planning?

An image of a marathon sprang to mind. I am not a marathon runner by any means. (Nor am I necessarily interested in becoming one anytime soon!) However, a few weeks ago, I had experienced a marathon through the eyes of an avid runner.

One of my co-workers had invited our family to watch his wife run the White Rock Lake marathon near Dallas. As my brother and I waited at the finish line (along with several hundred other faithful friends and family members of the runners), I was amazed by what I saw. The excitement was palpable, as each exhausted runner crossed the finish line. Some panted with their hands on their hips as they downshifted to a walking pace. Others literally slowed and fell into the arms of their waiting loved ones who embraced them and cheered.

From my vantage point, I could see the runners making their way to the finish line for at least half a mile. As they approached the last leg of their journey, their faces showed that all of them were in the zone. Nothing else mattered except crossing that finishing line. A giant digital clock nearby counted off tenths of seconds, and some of them had their eye on that second hand, desperately hoping to beat their best time. Yet the majority just seemed focused on taking the next step forward. The rest of the runners around them didn't even seem to exist. It was intense - and I was just observing all of it from the sidelines! I talk to people about their values and goals all day long. In my line of work, you quickly realize how much easier it is for people to make smart choices - with their money and with their lives - when they have a clear picture of their ultimate goal. I am constantly amazed by the power of a clearly defined goal and choosing to get on the path toward that objective. In all my years of business, I had seldom seen a group of people so focused - channeling every last bit of energy they had, to achieve success - until that day at the marathon. As I drove home, one thought dominated my thoughts: *What would it take to run 26 miles?*

Twenty-six miles is a long time to keep running. However, it became clear to me that day that a marathon is actually a lot longer than just the 26 miles on pavement. I was stationed at the finish line, but my thoughts kept going back to the moment the race started. In a race, all the attention focuses on the finish line and who breaks the tape first, but I realized that the starting line was in some ways just as important. The starting line for these runners began a lot further back than just a piece of tape stretched across a street 26 miles earlier.

It stretched back several months, maybe even a year or more. The day they first made the decision to run a marathon, long before the starting gun fired on the day of the race. The race actually began with that first desire. It began the moment the alarm sounded in the darkness on the very first morning of training.

Likewise, the finish line represented more than the end of a long race. It was a celebration of hundreds of hours they had spent training and preparing before race day, fulfilling a long-range plan to succeed. It occurred to me watching these runners that anything worth doing in life begins the same way - with desires and goals followed by a plan and the passion to achieve them. Michael Gerber writes in his book, *The E-Myth,* about the surprising reason that most small businesses/personal goals fail. It's not because their dream is too big, but rather too small and too realistic. They aren't big enough to sustain more life.

We have to see clearly where we want to go, envision what it feels like to achieve that goal and plan our way backwards. Every successful runner has clearly envisioned what crossing the finish line would feel like *before* they ever set foot on pavement. They have already felt the utter excitement, the glorious thrill, the incomparable feeling of strength and invincibility. That's the vision that drives them to come up with a plan - whatever it takes - to experience all that moment holds in store. You run a race from *start to finish*; but first you must envision it from *finish to start* and figure out all the steps it will take to get you where you want to be.

With these ideas churning in my head, I set aside the speech I'd rehearsed, took a deep breath and opened with the illustration of running the White Rock Lake marathon. Then I asked, "What does it take to run a marathon?"

The students started firing off answers. *New shoes, eating right, athletic shorts, a running coach.* Fifty different answers came flying across the room: *"Start slowly; Build a timeline; Exercise."* About the time that some of the students probably started wondering what a marathon had to do with a career in finance anyway, I asked them, "So. What is your 26 miles?"

The room became very quiet.

I issued the challenge again, "What is *your 26* miles?"

Here were all these students on the threshold of a new beginning with the whole world open to them. They could run any "marathon" (a metaphor for what they wanted most out of life) that they wanted to run. Some would run it in their hometown: working in the financial industry, marrying, having children and buying their first home. Some would graduate and move to join a financial firm possibly in Dallas, New York or Boston and begin a life there. As they anxiously paced the starting line of a brand new life as soon-to-be college graduates, I wanted them to consider their goals carefully and picture the next finish line in their lives.

More importantly, I wanted them to visualize an important life goal and then start tracing back what it would take to get them there. I challenged them to realize that no matter what vision they had for their lives at that moment, once they had a specific destination in mind, they could begin their 26 miles. Every step they took toward this goal would count. (Incidentally, I had two students tell me that they wanted to run a real marathon after that!)

WHAT IS YOUR 26 MILES?

So, what is your 26 miles? What specific goals do you want to achieve in your lifetime? Those things that keep you up at night thinking, *"If money and practicality were not considerations, I'd be doing this right now . . ."* Can you see clearly what it will take for you to break the tape at that finish line? Or did you turn thirty, or forty or fifty and decide the race was over for you? Whatever your goals are for your life, can you envision everything you will have to do in order to make them happen? That's where developing a passion for the possibilities in life begins. And it has no age limits. *The great thing about dreams is that they have no expiration date.*

Once you create a goal and stretch the tape across the finish line in your mind, you begin to deal with everything else in your life from a new perspective. You start to figure out how all of your activities, endeavors, relationships and priorities relate to achieving that goal.

This kind of inner vision springs from a burning desire to convert a dream into reality and turn dedication into success. It comes from passion. You have to be passionate about the unexplored possibilities in your life. If you have no desire to be or do more in your life, you probably can't see any goals on the horizon worth pursuing. The truth is, some people have this passion and others just don't. But where does it come from? And if we suspect that we weren't born with it - then what?

Seeing The Possibilities

Most people say, "Seeing is believing." We've got it wrong. If you choose to believe it first, *then* your eyes will be open to seeing the possibilities. What do we truly believe about our ability to do the impossible? Our lives are primarily shaped by the foundational beliefs we bought into as children. Sometimes what we envision for our lives is limited because people convince us from an early age that we can't do certain things or become certain people. And we agree.

Somewhere along the way, we allow someone or something to smother the flame of possibility in our lives. We all begin with grand ideas and a belief that we can achieve almost anything. However, life begins to erode most of us at some point with its routines and demands, not to mention all the 'can't do' language we are fed.

Our focus starts to slip and, along with it, many of our dreams.

I felt the first flicker of possibility in the tenth grade when an insurance agent came to my house to discuss auto insurance with my parents. My parents are both deaf mutes and I was interpreting for them. I remember sitting across the table from him and admiring his ability to help families with key decisions. More importantly, I understood that by helping my family think wisely about our future and implement a well-organized plan, he was putting us in touch with the ability to dream and to make dreams happen. I didn't necessarily want to be in the insurance business, but I knew after that night that I wanted to help people make wise decisions about the areas of their lives that were important to them.

Running The Rat Race Or Your Race

You may have started your 26-mile marathon a long time ago with the finish line clearly in view. You had goals. Dreams. Ideas. And then something happened.

Maybe you got distracted along the way by the stuff of life - changing jobs, marrying, moving cross-country, having kids, paying a mortgage, etc. You lost sight of the goal and now life is just kind of dragging you along. You are not living your life on purpose because you honestly no longer believe that everything is possible. When we cease to *believe* that everything is possible, we can no longer see it happening. The dream fades. Sometimes it even seems to disappear from view. When that happens, instead of steadily running a marathon toward our greater goals and dreams, we end up running a directionless race without a goal or dream in sight.

If this is you, you are not alone. Many people find themselves on the sidelines. It's been so long since they actively pursued their goals that they're now more comfortable amid the spectators than those sweating it out in the race of life.

Have you noticed that spectators look and act differently than those in the race? They're dressed differently for one thing. They don't look like runners with their jeans and Saturday-morning sweatshirts, whereas people in the race have their game on. They *strip* down to the necessities for hitting their goal - shorts, shirt and shoes. People in the crowd are relaxed and casual, cupping their lattes and talking and laughing with each other as the minutes turn into hours. By contrast, those in the race count every minute, and they have an intensity in their eyes that has long been missing in the crowd.

Ask a runner in the middle of a marathon what is most important to him or her. You will get a definitive answer. The runners know without a doubt what is most important to them. Ask the crowd, and you're more likely to meet with hesitation. Ask it again and you might see a mix of looks between wistful defeat and glimmers of hope. Those who do not know what they want out of life have no lens of enthusiasm through which to envision the journey from start to finish. Are you in the crowd, or are you in the race?

SHARING YOUR DREAM WITH OTHERS

If you began training for a marathon tomorrow, you could read books and pore over magazines about basic training for marathons, but that would only get you so far. You'd have to actually get in there and start running to make it happen. And what if you missed an important step? What if you started to go off course?

Anyone who is serious about attaining a goal reaches a critical turning point when they realize that they can no longer go it alone. They have to assemble a team that is willing to support their dream with passion. A focused group that sees the biggest picture possible and can help them figure out every single thing that needs to take place all the way to the finish line. For a runner, this team might include other running partners, a nutritionist or a coach. Friends and family members may be on the sidelines cheering them on. These people keep the athlete's eyes on the road when his or her focus starts to slip, continually charting the course toward the final goal.

Another strategic part of your 26 miles is surrounding yourself with success. Begin studying successful people in your community. Make their acquaintance. Examine their talents and achievements. You will undoubtedly uncover a support team of people standing behind the curtain. No successful person arrives at that place by themselves. They all needed a team to help them get there.

You have to actively seek others to help you construct the game plan and keep you on track. Hopefully, that's one of the reasons you picked up this book. Achieving the impossible is not just about achieving all that you can imagine for yourself; it's about creating and accessing allies who will motivate and assist you at critical points along the way. In fact, I devoted a whole chapter in this book to "Surrounding Yourself with People Who Motivate" (Chapter 10).

There are plenty of resources. Look for key people who know you, love you and want the best for you. Good friends and close family members who believe in you. Church groups and community organizations, teachers, mentors and life coaches. Chances are some of them will know at least one person who could play a key part in your success. Your team is one of the most crucial choices you will ever make. Wisely chosen, these people will help you take your life all the way to the top.

Of course, others can only be as enthusiastic about your dream as you are. If you are passionate and can "see" it happening in your future, they will believe in it, too. This chapter is about "seeing the impossible" take place in your life. I have found that there are key steps related to what I need to "see" to achieve what I want:

You have to constantly envision where you're going, "feel" the picture and never lose sight.

You have to see success happening in your future.

You have to see (and eliminate) the self-imposed limits hindering your success.

Envision Where You're Going and Never Lose Sight of the Goal

The first step in any race is to envision where you're going and plot the journey to that destination. Athletes are single-mindedly focused on the goal at hand. Even when they're training for a local track meet or a state championship—they always have something like the Olympics in mind. The grand picture. They always focus on the ultimate goal. Everything else is subordinate to that ideal.

In my own race, I always dreamed of making a global difference in kids' lives. One of the steps along the way was being elected onto the school board by the age of 29. That way I knew I could make choices that would impact kids positively. I came from a lower income family and figured out early on that education was the only way out. I always wanted to motivate and encourage people to be the best version of themselves. In its own way, this book is a step fulfilled, another way for me to impact or energize a life. And selfishly, that energizes me.

I had to learn the strategies for ignoring the fluff and overcoming challenges and distractions that threatened to take me off course. That way I could pursue what was truly important to me. I needed a team of people to plug in to help me uncover my values, strengths and desires in order to design a realistic, yet ambitious plan for attaining those goals.

I also had to learn to hold the vision I had in my mind. Yogi Berra, in one of his head-scratching Yogi-ism's, said, "You've got to be careful, if you don't know where you're going, because you might not get there."

Seeing Success Happening in Your Future

I used to coach Little League football. Being in charge of 26 little kids running around with helmets so big they looked like bobble heads is quite a challenge! I remember one game when I huddled up with the offense to call the next play. Suddenly I heard a little sniffle that rapidly escalated into muffled sobbing. My center had started crying in the middle of the huddle. I looked in his eyes and saw that he was scared of the bigger kids on the other team.

He was a little guy (all my guys were little), and he wasn't sure he wanted to go back to the line of scrimmage and play. I took him aside and I said, "Look. I know you're scared, and those other guys are a lot bigger than you. But you're smart. And smart beats strong." He kind of nodded his head and sniffed loudly again, but I could see the doubt in his eyes.

I knelt down on one knee and explained that he had an advantage over the others because he knew the snap count. "If you know when the snap count is," I told him, "then all you need to do is screen the defensive guy from getting to where you know the ball is going. See? Smart beats strong." When I told him that he had the advantage because of what he knew, his face began to light up. He saw himself doing exactly what I described. And winning. It gave him the strategy and vision he needed to succeed. And he did.

He was eight years old at the time, but he had raw talent even at that young age. Something told me that if we hadn't had this little talk, he would have quit that day and never picked up a football again. Ten years later, this same kid became a great athlete and played middle linebacker for Texas A&M University.

Instead of picturing all that can go wrong, see yourself successfully making the leap from where you are now to where you want to be. Imagine what it looks like to thrive. Picture yourself excelling.

Maybe it's been a long time since you experienced success in your personal life and you've forgotten what that feels or looks like. Maybe you've never known what it's like to reach for something beyond what you think you can attain—and achieve it. For most people that idea is a little intimidating. Fear of failure and nagging uncertainty about our futures are just two of the scavengers that eat away at our dreams and slyly keep us from daring to be, do and have more in our lives. Chase those parasites away! Envision yourself already there.

I learned a long time ago that doubt is the biggest enemy, not fear. *Doubt is the father of all negative emotions and the thief that steals our dreams and makes us play it safe.* We think that if we are sure about our vision and destination people will find us cocky or refer to us as smart alecks. Doubt pulls out the worst in us and steals the magnificent. Doubt says, "It's impossible. Can't be done." I learned a long time ago to make doubt my ally, and I learned a strange truth about him. Doubt holds a secret in his hands because he is the guardian of the gates to all miracles. He asks to be overcome and by overcoming him, he makes way for new rules, new records and new limits. He is the wise guardian that challenges the very best in us to step forward and say, "I respect you, I know your value and I am moving past you."

Identifying and Eliminating the Limits Hindering Your Success

You have to see success in your future, but at the same time identify the obstacles or limits that threaten to keep it from becoming reality.

What holds you back in life? Once you identify your limits, you can turn them into strengths.

There is an entire field of science devoted to doing this for athletes. Scientists study repetitive training sports such as running and cycling and their impact on the human body. For example, repetitive motions in a runner's stride can lead to imbalances in the muscles and leave him or her vulnerable to injury.

A runner's calves and hamstrings tighten and become very strong after thousands of miles of training, while the quadriceps gradually weaken. Professional sports trainers can conduct what they call a biomechanical evaluation to help identify any imbalances an athlete has in terms of alignment, flexibility and strength. They can then recommend specific stretches and strengthening exercises to minimize damage or imbalances - problems the runner likely never even knew he or she had.

We all have blind spots; at work, at school and in our personal lives. We need an honest evaluation of how we're doing in the areas of our lives that matter most. How can you improve if you don't know what's wrong?

In the area of finances, it could be that you ought to run at a different "financial pace" because you're spending beyond your means. It could be that you are running too slowly in the area of savings and it's time to speed up. You may be developing bad habits and financial patterns that could hurt you or others down the road.

Anyone can benefit from an outsider's analysis of his or her life. What would a professional analysis reveal about other areas of your life? Your job performance at work? Your marriage? Your interaction with co-workers or the people you're leading?

MOVING FROM SEEING IT TO PLANNING IT

Once you see in your mind who you want to be, what you want to do and what you want to have, you can work your way back from that desired future to create a plan for achieving it. The good news is that it's never too late!

Author Steven Covey calls this approach to our goals, "beginning with the end in mind." It means being focused on where you are headed in life so that you can take each step toward that future goal with purpose and passion now. Remember, the key to running a successful race is to see it from finish to start. The course of the race has its ups and downs. However, nothing can put us off once we have the goal clearly in view. We learn that even the downs are just part of the journey.

If you first see your goal and picture yourself taking the necessary steps for achieving success, you will undoubtedly achieve all that you can imagine. Once you see it, the next question then becomes: How do you do it? Simple. It's called creating a plan.

CHAPTER Two

PLANNING AND ACHIEVING YOUR GREATEST GOALS

STEP-BY-STEP

They came into my office holding a check from an oil and gas lease. This couple, older clients with our firm, had saved for years but had no formal financial plan. They also had no idea if they were "safe" or not. When they came to us, I sat with them and really listened. Together we identified their dreams and goals. Within a short time, we'd customized a master plan that structured their financial affairs. Just *how* well-organized their finances were now, would only become apparent to them later on - in fact, the day that they walked into my office holding that check.

I could see by the look on their faces that this was just a routine deposit into another investment, to keep them safe. They'd done well financially, but they'd forgotten the purpose of that plan. Goals reached, dreams to be fulfilled.

Ironically, the couple in this story was actually exactly where they wanted to be financially because they had been diligently following the financial plan we had created together. However, up to this point they had never taken time to celebrate, create memories and enjoy life—the very things that financial stability allows us to do.

Sitting across from them at the table that day, I looked up and asked, "Why don't you take this money and go on a trip of a lifetime?" They looked at each other wide-eyed and turned to look back at me.

"Could we?" the man asked doubtfully and scratched his chin. His wife looked from her husband to me and back to her husband in disbelief.

I showed them again where they were financially. Everything had been accomplished according to plan. Now it was time for them to begin enjoying the fruits of a diligent plan. I'm happy to say, that two months later they were taking pictures in front of the Opera House in Sidney, Australia.

ENJOYING THE ADVENTURE

The greatest enjoyment in my career is helping people plan for and experience a great life. When I ask people what having a great life means to them, I hear a number of different answers. Some want to be wealthy and have the freedom to invest in the future of others. Some want to have an intimate family life. Some want to travel. Others want security for them and their families. It doesn't matter what religion, ethnicity, background or nationality defines us, we all have a common desire to experience inner peace and know without a doubt that we've had some kind of impact on the world. I have one caveat along the way. Sometimes life brings us unplanned surprises, and in their own way they are just as important as planning a great life. Sometimes they are the rewards that keep us focused.

In my business, a lot of what we do begins with helping others re-discover for themselves what is most important to them. They know it; they just forgot it along the way. For me, it's just as important to design the steps as it is to design the goal.

Everyone has ideas and values that are sacred—things that never fail to make them smile, bring a sigh of relief or dare to dream. These are the steps that keep us on track with the bigger picture. Sometimes we think we have to wait "until something falls into place" for those to happen. Not always.

Recently a father and son sat down in my office to talk about the inheritance the teenager had received. He wanted to save for the future. I asked the son, "What is important about money to you?"

"Being secure," he answered cautiously and then his eyes lit up. "I always did want to visit the Smithsonian," he blurted out and then subsided again.

His father leaned forward and looked at his son. "What did you say?" he asked. "The Smithsonian?"

"I've always, *always* wanted to go to the Smithsonian," the son replied. A different kid was sitting in front of me now, his eyes bright with excitement.

Dumbfounded, the dad looked at his teenage son. "Son," he said, "I never knew you wanted to do that." They invested the money wisely, but there was a light in the father's eyes that had not been there before.

Three weeks later, they returned from a father-and-son trip to the Northeast that they would never forget. Their story reminds me that we all need to talk to each other about what we most want to do and experience in life. Those are the things we should share with one another. All too often we bury the things that are most important. The more you dream and share what you're going to do with the precious gift of life, the further you are likely to go.

Great Lives Take Planning

Unfortunately, many people's plans for a great life don't get off the ground because they are too busy to take the time to think through what they really want out of life. Many actually have to stop and reflect when I ask them what is most important to them.

It's astonishing how hard it is sometimes to write down the goals that are important to you. Even putting something like a simple timeline on our goals can be a new exercise for some people. Putting it on paper makes it real, creates confidence, eliminates negativity and convinces your subconscious mind that you can accomplish whatever you set out to do.

Unfortunately, we don't learn this early on in life. In school, we rarely teach children how to manage their time, money and other resources to help them achieve their dreams.

Most people live life saying, "If I had this, I could be that." That's not true. I have found that when you learn to "be" the person you want to be, or "be" the company you want to be and "do" the things you have to do in order to make that happen, then you'll "have" what you want to have. In that order.

We're taught not to dream too big or reach too high. *Don't set yourself up for disappointment. Don't bite off more than you can chew.* Don't. Don't. Don't. Soon "Don't" becomes "What's the use?" and we stop having any sort of plan for our lives. We just let life happen. We get jobs and soon forget about having a passion for careers or dreams. We don't think we should love our work, and we tend to lose sight of what we're really working for anyway.

Many people stop dreaming at the point of money. It doesn't take *money* to fuel your dreams. *Time* is the primary currency that powers our dreams. The root cause of not achieving them is failing to use your time wisely. Time is your primary currency for success; focus is second; money is last. The wise and diligent application of all three equals success.

In other words, a great life doesn't just happen on its own. You have to plan for it. Don't miss the unimaginably large rewards of disciplined planning as you push forward into the realm of all that your life could be. Spend a moment reflecting on and planning your dreams before you spend a dollar. The wise investment of your time will yield a more profitable return.

THE TRUTH ABOUT GOALS

Before you start capturing some of your goals on paper, you need to know what constitutes a good one.

Goals Are Not The Same As Desires

Goals represent those things over which you have personal control; desires are simply what you would *like* for the outcome to be. Some people confuse the two. You might say one of your goals in life is to raise great kids. However, something that requires someone else to conform to your wishes is not a good goal. Instead, that would be more of a desire. Desires often require someone else to help fulfill them. What if your kids make decisions you don't like? What if they choose a path other than the one you have in mind for them?

Be sure that the goals you have for your life do not involve the desire to change someone else's. We have no permission to change other people. At the most, we have the power to initiate real change when someone sees us accomplish our own goals and feels inspired to want more out of life, too. Whatever you choose to be, do or have - regardless of others' behavior - is a true goal.

A Goal Must Tap Into Your Passions

One of the most important questions I ask people about their life goals is: "How will you feel once you have accomplished them?" If that person is not energetic about accomplishing his or her goals, it's either too small, or plain unexciting.

If you can't get in touch with the feelings you would experience once you accomplish your life goals, you won't have the fuel (passion) to achieve them. Most of us run out of gas way before we reach our destination. It's not that our dreams are too big - it's that they're too small! Worse still, we forget to tank up on a regular basis to keep the vehicle moving.

I often ask people to tell me why achieving their goals is important `to them so they can tap into their passion. I believe the following formula is true: ***Discovering Why - Creates More Passion - Fulfills Goals.*** For example, we all know it's important to save money and have enough to meet our needs. However, we all have different opinions on why that is important to us. Knowing why creates more passion for fulfilling our goals.

Knowing *why* we want to save money will reveal what drives us. Some people are driven to earn and save money because of past experience. I've had people tell me, "I was poor when I was growing up and I never want to go there again." Think about why you have certain goals for your life, and you'll begin to understand what you're passionate about and what drives you forward. You'll also begin to realize that for each of us, "money" is a synonym for a variety of freedoms.

A Goal is personal and sacrosanct

For me, it's important that the goals I have are things I want to achieve, not what others expect of me. Constantly worrying about what everybody expects would short-circuit my ability to establish big goals. I'd have too many aspects to consider, and I'd probably shut down. Life goals are inviolable rights. Within the dreamer lies the place where happiness and "can do" is alive and well.

If you go into a career that you didn't choose and didn't want, no wonder you don't feel passionate about it. You have to pursue what you love to do in order to be able to set personal goals that bounce you out of bed every day because you are excited to get out there and take those goals another step further. I only pursue things I have a passion for doing in areas that highlight my strengths.

A Goal requires action

Many of us outline our goals but don't take any action to make them happen. That's like having the keys to a beautiful car that you never drive anywhere.

Some people don't take action because they're afraid they will fail. This kind of person figures a car in the garage is safer than a car in motion, so they never crank the engine. There will always be challenges and unforeseen obstacles. It's impossible to anticipate where the bottlenecks are until we start taking action. There's an old saying, "Do what you fear most and you control fear." Besides, most of what you fear happening only exists in your mind.

So what if you decide to do nothing? Inactivity is not as neutral as it sounds - it is a conscious decision to not move forward in our lives. When we take no action, we're going against the flow of life that naturally wants to move us forward and be, do and have more than we presently experience. It actually takes more energy to do nothing. It's like treading water - you're not going anywhere, but it still takes lots of time and energy to keep afloat.

I want to be more like the people you see at an airport. When I travel, I see people dressed for the beach and businessmen in power suits all boarding the same plane. One guy's shoving a beach bag into the overhead compartment next to a businesswoman balancing her computer and a month's worth of paperwork in her lap.

We may look different, but everybody in an airport has one thing in common: *they are all going somewhere.* From the business people in power suits to the vacationers heading to Bermuda, every person in the terminal is headed somewhere in their lives. They're either going somewhere on purpose, or they're letting life drag them along to the next thing. No one is standing still. We are all people in motion - either intentionally or reactively.

MAPPING • LIVING YOUR LIFE ON PURPOSE

In some ways, financial planning is similar to a charter travel agency - we help people plan or map the best route to desired destinations in their personal lives. People who have a passion for possibilities develop a clear vision for their lives and follow a map to get there.

Maps show us where we've been, where we are and, most importantly, where to go next. If you were driving from Texas to Indiana, you could look at a climate map, a topographical map and a resource map, but none of those maps would get you there. On a road trip, you use a highway map or road atlas to get to your destination.

The map matters! How we reach our destination depends on the clarity of the map we create. If you don't know where you are going, any map will take you there. Creating the right map or plan for your goals will prove strategic to your success.

People who believe in the power of possibilities are modern day cartographers - map-makers who chart their way to new, unexplored worlds and dimensions waiting patiently to be discovered in their lives.

A large part of our personal map relates to how we grew up. My map is different from yours. You are the exclusive author, discoverer and complier of that map, and only you know how it should look.

The Right Map Makes Your Priorities Clear

I've helped people create road maps for tangible goals like personal wealth, but the greater thrill is the byproduct of good maps that enhance the less tangible areas of our lives.

Take marriage relationships for example. A husband and wife sat in my office one day. He was a doctor, and they enjoyed a comfortable lifestyle. However, the husband was really frustrated by his wife's spending habits, and they were not communicating well about this issue.

We spent a lot of time talking about their dreams and what was important to them. They described wanting to plan for college for their children and maintaining a certain lifestyle at retirement. The wife shared how important it was to give to others and support good causes because of the peace of mind she gained by doing so. She also always wanted to be in a position to help her family when needed.

However, a glaring problem arose when we laid out the big game plan for their future. The wife's spending rate threatened those future goals. Credit card debt was mounting. Sitting in my office that day, she understood for the first time that her current actions would soon sabotage tomorrow's goals.

As the realization sank in, she sat up straight, looked each of us in the eye and asked for a pair of scissors. She then reached inside her purse, took eight credit cards out of her wallet and cut them to pieces on my

conference room table!

When we are committed to putting our plans on paper and living with purpose, everything in life dovetails. We can finally see the delicate balance of how every value we hold dear and every decision we make affects everything else.

Clear Vision Brings Easier Decisions

It's amazing what can happen when you clearly sculpt the vision and then just follow the plan. Roy Disney, Walt Disney's brother and co-founder of Disneyland, once said, "When your visions are clear, then your decisions are easy." Decisions become easier in all aspects of life.

To go back to the marathon, vision and decision-making is especially important for runners. You won't find serious marathon competitors thinking about what *else* they could be doing with their time. They are focused on one thing only - running.

They know they have to achieve certain benchmarks in a certain amount of time in order to meet their targets: Eat certain foods and avoid others, run a specific distance for a certain number of days in the week. These decisions follow their master plan. As a result, daily decisions come rather easily to them and, in time, they become second nature.

Motivated people "run" every day of their lives. It doesn't matter if it's raining outside. They don't stand at the door agonizing over the decision. They made the decision a long time ago before the first drop of rain ever fell: "I will run every day. No matter what." Therefore, all the rest of the decisions related to that one goal are easy. At the top of their to-do list every day is this notation:

To Do:

Decide when and where to run.

Go do it.

It's simple. Once you have clearly pictured *what* you want to achieve, deciding *how* to do it will come much more easily. After all, a plan is just a series of clearly defined decisions, executed one after the other.

For several years, our town hosted a golf tournament called The Eisenhower. Many professional golfers came, and it was an exciting time to meet them and socialize with everyone in the event. One year, I was standing near one of the greens with my wife and suddenly said to her, "Next year, we are going to be right in the middle of that, and I'm going to play in the Eisenhower."

Up to that point, I had rarely played golf. Make that almost never. Still, I saw myself out there on the greens next year. I just had no idea at that moment how I was going to do it. However, because I had a clear vision of what I wanted to do, my decisions about how to do it came easily. It was simply a matter of seeing my goal, coming up with a plan to achieve it and following it through.

The first decision I made was to sign up the very next week for golf lessons so I wouldn't kill anybody! (I'd always wanted to learn how to play golf, but people always said it would be a lot more fun if I could actually find my ball.) Before my first lesson, I had to decide what kind of shoes to buy, what clubs to use and what clothing I would need for the course. I took baby steps toward that goal, and a year later I reached a 13 handicap and played in the Eisenhower. Much to my family's surprise, I stuck with it, too. I'm right at a 10 handicap today.

Once people "get" the power of discovering what's most important to them and creating a step-by-step plan to achieve it, things begin to fall into place. First, their energy and enthusiasm spikes. Suddenly they begin reaching key destinations in their lives. Spending more time with family and friends and less time slogging at the office. Expanding their personalities into the people they envisioned they could be. Deepening their relationships with others.

They develop a heightened sense of their own personal values and begin making important decisions based on those values, aligning themselves with other people who share the same goals. These people start creating the lives they've dreamed of living.

SO, WHERE DO YOU START?

I see another common thread in the lives of my clients' who are just beginning to put their plans into action. They want to do it all! By themselves. Right now! That's just the opposite of what needs to happen.

You see, most people realize that following a plan of action means creating an order in which to accomplish their goals. The newer clients know that there are things they must do. However, they don't realize that there are also things you must stop doing, and those must become a part of your plan as well. Some activities have to be reduced or eliminated, and some have to be delegated so you are free to pursue what is most important. It's also important to learn when you need to do things yourself and when to team with others.

Three

TRUSTING OTHERS AND DOING MORE TOGETHER

To return once again to the analogy of the runner preparing to run a marathon, the question is not only, "What will you *do* to get ready to run your 26 miles?" but "What will you need to *stop* doing in order to achieve it?"

If you don't understand this important principle, you might feel overwhelmed by the idea of making changes because you'll view change as adding a whole new set of activities and responsibilities to your already busy life. *When will you find the time? How will you balance it with your other responsibilities?* Instead of making your life easier and more efficient and effective, you'll perceive possibilities as a burden, not a blessing.

REFINING YOUR TO-DO LIST

With the marathon in mind, let's say that you decide to start by running two miles, three to five times a week. You work a full day at home or at the office, arrange dinner, get your children to soccer practice, pick up around the house or yard, help the kids do homework until bedtime and then crash into bed yourself - only to wake up and do the same thing all over again tomorrow.

Without making any adjustments to your already crammed schedule, you'll be frazzled and frustrated by the end of the first week! Instead, you have to make room for a new and positive lifestyle. We often think of delegating as a principle related to tasks at the office. However, it should apply to many areas of our lives.

What could you *stop* doing (tasks that can be delegated) that would make room in your life for something you want to *start* doing? Maybe you spend an hour a week taking your kids back and forth to soccer practice. Join a car pool with other soccer moms. Defer some household chores to family members to free up an extra forty-five minutes to an hour. Create or join a supper club and delegate a meal or two each week among a group of friends.

We have to curb the impulse to do everything ourselves, if we want to free up space for our goals. The power of delegation is amazing, if you use it properly.

YOUR QUALITY OF LIFE MATTERS

There are some things in our lives that we must delegate and some things that we simply have to do ourselves. You can delegate your tax preparation to an expert, but you can't delegate a Saturday morning aerobics class to someone else to do for you just so that you can check it off your list. Likewise, you can't delegate the practice of your personal faith or religion. And you cannot delegate fun. (If you could, I'd say to delegate it to me and I'll have all the fun possible for both of us!) However, there are things that you *can* and should delegate if you want to reach your goals.

I worked with a coffee-loving client whose greatest desire was to spend more time with her kids. She was a professional career woman, trying to juggle the responsibilities of being a mom and running the household. After working a full week, she would clean the house on Saturday mornings - do laundry and other chores she couldn't tackle Monday through Friday.

However, what she most wanted to do on Saturday mornings was spend quality time with her boys. We have a tool we use in my practice called a Quality of Life Enhancer. It basically asks people to complete an exercise to help them see what would increase the quality of their lives.

Once she completed the exercise, she began to see a disparity between what was most important to her (her values) and what she was actually doing with her time. Spending more time with her children would definitely reflect her values and increase her quality of life. However, she felt as though her time was not her own. She told herself that she could not delegate the household chores to someone else because she could not afford the extra $100 out of the family budget. She felt torn.

It was clear that spending the most time possible with her family was the number one goal in her life and it lined up with her personal values. I asked what it would take to get there. She had been envisioning the $100 as an extra expense, but I challenged her to make her coffee at home instead of stopping at the coffee store every day. The expense disappeared. This is an example of prioritizing. The return on her adjustment would be a gain of several hours a week with her boys.

So many times we live like this single mom did - feeling like what we want out of life is unattainable . . . impossible. Just the opposite of possibility-thinking. We run out of hope when we run out of possibilities. We have to do something radical to break out of that thought pattern. Fortunately, my client did and it revolutionized her home life.

She realized that she could not delegate time with her boys to someone else. No one else could replace her sitting beside them at the breakfast table talking. However, she could delegate the housework. And she did. What seemed like a sacrifice at first reaped more dividends than she could have imagined.

It's possible to experience more happiness and fulfillment in our lives and in our family if we learn to prioritize. There will always be much more that needs to be done than we can do ourselves. We have to learn to distinguish between what only we can do from what should be passed on to others.

FACT AND FICTION

To learn how to delegate tasks and responsibilities and increase our quality of life, we have to get serious about certain false beliefs or misconceptions we've bought into. We all have misunderstandings surrounding the concept of delegating; otherwise, we'd do it more often.

> **MISCONCEPTION:** "I'm the only one who can do what I do."
>
> **TRUTH:** Look around carefully—if you weren't there, someone else could take the load.

I've seen people accept all the responsibility for a task because they are convinced there is no one else to do it. In fact, this belief is so strong that they never even *ask* if someone else can or will help! It happens in organizations, and I've seen it at work in families.

In families, it may look something like this. Parents reach a certain age where they need help taking care of themselves. "Bob" sees that his parents need increased care, so he assumes full responsibility for the task at hand. At first, he feels really needed and important as the sole caregiver. As the eldest, he'd always assumed this responsibility would fall to him anyway. (Although this has never been discussed among the siblings. This is just Bob's assumption.)

Over time, however, he feels pressured by the increasing time commitment - driving his parents to medical appointments and keeping all their medication straight. He had no idea it would be this exhausting. The parents feel guilty, but Bob assures them it's fine.

Only . . . it's not.

Soon, he begins to envy his siblings' lifestyle, footloose and fancy free while he's "doing all the work" caring for *their* parents. Every time his sister sends photos from their most recent Cancun family vacation, he feels resentful. He starts to feel like someone owes him something. However, he has never asked for help from his siblings, nor has he let them know how much of a burden it is on his own family. The siblings are pleased that mom and dad seem to be doing so well. They never give Bob's silent anguish a second thought.

Eventually his resentment boils over. Suddenly there is a family rift between the siblings that no one but Bob ever saw coming.

The dynamic here is pretty simple. Many times we unintentionally put ourselves in positions of stress and anxiety because we don't ask for help. We see what needs to be done and we take over. People who have not learned the power of delegation sit with the problem and the solution in their own hands. They don't realize that a good part of the reason for their anger and resentment is their own unwillingness to share the load - to delegate. All of their energy is directed toward everything that they are doing alone, versus all the missed opportunities to share the burden. It's a volatile recipe for ruined relationships.

When an organization is led along similar lines, it's the same story, different verse. Whether we're the president of an organization or head of our department and we don't delegate properly, or set clear expectations, things soon begin to break down.

Our natural inclination is to grab back all of the responsibility and do it all ourselves. In doing so, we compound the mess by failing to recognize the very thing that set the disaster in motion. Our inability to delegate! Leo Tolstoy once observed, "Everyone thinks of changing the world, but no one thinks of changing himself."

In some ways, large or small, we contribute to the effect in everything. If we experience a great outcome in a certain situation, we know when we did something positive that contributed to the effect of that outcome. If it's a negative outcome, we should also look inside first - not look for someone else to blame.

Most disappointments can be traced to one of a few causes. Either we:

1. Give others a task that they're not qualified to do, or;

2. They don't accept the responsibility or;

3. Our definition of the expectations is unclear.

Will Rogers said, "If you never want to be disappointed, don't expect too much." People who don't delegate, end up doing everything themselves in order to avoid being disappointed. Some people are afraid to delegate in case they lose control and wind up looking bad. They delegate as little as possible and exhaust themselves, even though others are willing to help. Once we start to develop that mentality, we're in trouble.

In families, relationships suffer. In companies, the bottom line suffers. Delegating gives you more time, energy and resources to accomplish the things on your list that are both important and that you're gifted at doing.

Don't try telling this to those who refuse to delegate. They are utterly convinced that taking their hands off a project will harm the end goal. Conversely, things could go better if they would learn to communicate and delegate.

> MISCONCEPTION: No one else wants the responsibilities I handle.
>
> TRUTH: People like rising to new challenges, as long as they understand the expectations.

How will you know what talents you have on your team unless you are willing to give them new opportunities? Highly motivated people are lifelong learners. They are interested in every aspect of their company, including other roles not necessarily related to their primary job. A company may have the best salesperson right under their nose. Only that top salesperson is presently misplaced as the new receptionist who is dying to get into sales.

Delegating is a superb way to uncover hidden talent. Hoarding responsibilities stunts everyone's growth. You can't honestly say, "No one wants my responsibilities" until you've clearly explained what you're doing and offered someone else a chance to try it. Communicate your needs, set the expectations and unleash the potential talent.

I've noticed that any time I have a new hire, that person is always better than the person I had before. Why is that? Is the job changing? No, the general responsibilities stay much the same. Are better people coming to my door? Maybe. I rather think that it has more to do with the fact that I'm learning how to be a better employer and set clearer expectations.

With every hire, I know more about what I want, and that makes it easier for a new person to deliver the goods.

You can see how this relates to families. Imagine a mother picking up dirty socks and wet towels off the bathroom floor for the thirty-seventh time that week. As she stuffs another sock into the laundry hamper, she mutters, "I'm the one who has to do everything. Nobody around here wants to do the dirty work."

It's just so tempting to play the role of the martyr and take it all on ourselves, when all we have to do is explain the family expectations in a way that everyone "gets" their part. What if she went to her husband and children, sat them down on the couch and together they laid out a new plan instead, where everyone became responsible for doing part of the family laundry?

There are certain things you are especially gifted at accomplishing. These are the things you can and should be doing. However, there are just as many tasks and responsibilities that may be important, but for which you have no gift or time. If you learn how to delegate what shuts you down emotionally and physically, you will increase your effectiveness ten-fold.

Still think no one wants your responsibilities? How do you know until you ask? Keeping the show running doesn't have to mean you're running the show.

> MISCONCEPTION: "I have to do everything myself if I
>   want it done right."
>
> TRUTH: Others can do it as well as you can. Sometimes
>   even better

If you're convinced that no one can perform a responsibility or contribute to an idea as well as you can, you might question your leadership skills. This applies to employers and team leaders who are accountable for the personal and professional development of their team. It also applies to parents whose main job is to grow their children into responsible adults.

Part of what determines our approach to delegating to other people are our beliefs about them, which form our expectations. The same goes for our children. If we believe we have smart, talented children, we'll expect more out of them and give them tasks that challenge their potential. And guess what happens with children whose parents believe they are smart, talented and responsible? They usually turn out to be exactly that. Children, like our other relationships, rise to meet our expectations of them.

What man goes to work and says to himself, "I hope I get to mess something up today?" What child thinks, "I hope I do something today to disappoint my parents?" Deep down, everyone longs to do an extraordinary job and belong. We just have to draw it out of them.

My maternal grandfather used to always say positive things about us as kids. He would dish out compliments and encouragement as if he were handing out fistfuls of candy. "They're smart boys," he would say about my brother John and I. "You're going to do something with your life." He ranted and raved about so many positive things in our lives. No wonder we loved having him around. Someone else's confidence in you can change your life. Your confidence in someone else can change theirs!

Of course, there are those who don't seem to believe that other people are gifted beyond average intelligence. We know that by the way they hoard the most important tasks and responsibilities. Then a sad thing happens. After a while, the people closest to them begin to doubt their own abilities. Their minds and talents atrophy like muscles they never get to use.

We need more people at work and at home like my grandfather.

We need people who entice the best out of others by simply tuning into their "can-do" side. If you want to enhance your team's skills, don't take away important tasks—demonstrate confidence in them by giving them more. Increase your child's self-esteem by entrusting him or her with responsibilities around the house. Your confidence in other people can amplify their skills in dramatic ways.

There is a specific way to demonstrate confidence in others when giving them a task. Clarify the outcome you desire and then step away from their process.

In my office, one of the main objectives for my team is to make clients feel loved and appreciated. I can't tell my team exactly how to do it or it will come across as less than sincere. If I've done my job right, I will have 10 different employees making sure clients feel the love 10 different ways. Each team member will use their individual talents to do it. Conventional wisdom suggests that you should build a step-by-step process that everybody could follow. Smart delegation requires me to explain the outcome I want and then allow them to find their own ways to accomplish it. Not everybody's personality can fit one process because everyone is different.

A single person tackling a project will come up with one scenario. However, two or three people can create what I like to think of as a *mastermind group* that is able to churn out ideas and solutions at a faster rate and better quality. That's called synergy. It plays to everyone's strengths, wisdom and experience. Sure, you are free to do everything yourself - but don't think that's the only way it can be done right. It's just that it will be done the way that *you* think is right.

If you have doubts about the power of delegation, take an extended vacation. Find out what gets done without you being around.

There is a big, old cemetery in the middle of the city where I live. On either side are heavily trafficked streets filled with everyday activities. The gravestones tell the names of many people who were convinced that life would fall apart and grind to a halt if they didn't do whatever it is they used to do. It's a sober reminder about feeling absolutely irreplaceable.

LEARNING TO DELEGATE AS A MATTER OF TRUST

It all comes down to a matter of trust. At the office, if a major project needs to be completed we'll either trust someone else to get it done - or we won't. At home, we'll either trust our spouse to help run the household or we won't.

Spouses often go back and undo everything the other did to resolve an issue. Imagine "Joey," a typical teenage boy, breaks curfew for the second time in a week. Father goes to Joey and grounds him for a week. "I wouldn't have done it that way," the wife thinks when she finds out what happened. She marches back into Joey's room and lifts the sentence that the father just imposed. Joey is thrilled, but the father feels frustrated and powerless. Trust has been violated.

Our level of trust indicates whether we are operating primarily out of fear *("Oh no! Someone else will mess it up if I let them do it")* or if we're learning to empower people by delegating. *("Great! I believe someone else can do an even better job than I can.")*

One of the highest compliments a client can give me is to hand me a hard-earned dollar. They're saying, "I trust you to manage this for me." I have never lost sight of that privilege. Nevertheless, I have also learned that if you want people to trust you, you must first be willing to demonstrate trust.

I understand that a lot of people come to the point where it's hard to trust others to help them. However, I've always believed that if one person out of 100 burns you doesn't mean the other 99 will follow suit.

The alternative is not trusting anybody, convinced that someone's out to get you. Imagine two wealthy children playing kick-ball in the street with less affluent kids nearby. The wealthy father says, "Don't play with them," creating a barrier. By instilling that small seed of mistrust and division in the heart of a child, he or she will grow up not knowing who to trust. It's a horrible thing to do. Still, many people (especially those who have been burned) think that others have to *earn* their trust first.

Trust people from the beginning until they "un-earn" it. That may go against conventional wisdom, but most people will reciprocate. You'll have a better relationship if you build in trust from the outset than if you waste time waiting for it to trickle in one drop at a time.

Most of us are told from childhood not to talk to strangers.

We should outgrow the warning when we become adults or we'll remain prisoners of our distrust. You may have heard the story about the little boy whose father said, "Whenever I'm not around, I don't want you to talk to strangers."

"But, Dad," the little boy responded, "If I don't talk to strangers, how do I make new friends?"

My parents were both born deaf mutes. As the eldest son, I grew up facilitating communication between them and a hearing world. Sometimes we were lost and needed directions. Sometimes we needed help getting into the right line. I grew up having to talk to strangers and trusting everybody! That mindset prepared me to relate to people on a similar level as an adult.

WHERE ARE YOU FOCUSED?

Consider the myriad of opportunities we gain when we shift our focus from the 1 in 100 people who will disappoint us to the 99 we can trust enough to share responsibilities and build our dreams together.

Possibilities shrink when you fixate on what's wrong with a person, situation or circumstance. Possibility-thinking focuses on what's good and asks, "How can I make it better?" Learning to improve and optimize who you are, what you do and what you have is fundamental to possibility thinking.

CHAPTER | *Four*

WINNING BY
A NOSE

Success is most often a "win by a nose." The phrase originated sometime in the mid-1800s to describe a horse race that was so close that only the nose of the winning horse came in ahead of another horse. The difference in prize money between the top two winning horses was staggering. However, the win itself was only by a small margin. In racing, one horse just has to be a little bit faster, a little better conditioned - and that extra little bit makes all the difference.

The Santa Anita Handicap in California, considered one of the most important wintertime races for thoroughbreds in North America, carries a top purse of one million dollars. In the thirties, a horse by the name of Seabiscuit captured the nation's attention as "the little horse that could" because he raced and won against horses twice his size.

However, Seabiscuit had never won at the famed Santa Anita Handicap. In fact, he suffered a frustrating loss on two prior occasions in 1937 and 1938 during what would prove to be extremely close races. Not long after his second defeat, Seabiscuit retired from horse racing due to injuries. Still, the idea of winning the Santa Anita lingered.

In 1940, too stubborn to quit, his team quietly made plans to enter the Santa Anita Handicap for a third time despite Seabiscuit's injuries. As the aging jockey put it, the horse and rider would race the final race of their career "with four good legs between us." Losing by a nose in the previous races inspired the horse and his rider to train a little longer and try a little harder this time. And to everyone's surprise, Seabiscuit won the legendary Hundred Grander, as the Santa Anita Handicap was then called, in style.

SUCCESS IS
WINNING BY A NOSE

Losing by a nose - not once, but twice - could have been a debilitating experience for Seabiscuit, his rider and owner. Some thought they were smart to call it quits. However, it had just the opposite effect on the team and actually motivated them to dig deep and secure a victory.

In life, we can miss success by such a narrow margin that if we had just pushed ourselves a little bit harder or thought through our strategy a little better, it would have resulted in a different outcome altogether. Like Seabiscuit, we can either allow adversity or disappointment to cripple us or inspire us to achieve even greater things.

On his first visit to Harrow, his former school grounds, in the fall of 1941, Winston Churchill delivered one of his most notable addresses to the students. With characteristic determination he told them, "This is the lesson: never give in, never give in, never, never, never, never - in nothing, great or small, large or petty . . . never yield to force; never yield to the apparently overwhelming might of the enemy."

Some people are so close to being, doing and having all that they can imagine, but they're either not willing or not able to put forth that little extra something and go all the way. So, they give in and let life's circumstances continue to beat them by a nose. Don't walk away when you could stay in one more round. Sometimes it's just a matter of doing one thing more or one thing different.

I remember a key employee who left my company in its infancy many years ago. I started my company operating out of my apartment as a college student. This colleague said that he was leaving because he thought another company would provide a better opportunity for growth. The fact that he used that phrase cut me to the core because we *were growing* at an incredible rate. I didn't believe anywhere or anything could provide a better opportunity for growth than what we were doing.

Once he left, I realized that I could mope around and try to figure out what it was that this guy saw in some other company that he didn't see in us, or I could use this deep disappointment as motivation for my own growth. I went straight out and earned several key financial consultant designations (CFP, CHFC, etc.). What should have taken me years to study and achieve took only eight months - I was that focused.

When I think about my life and the lives of other successful people, I realize that success is often really just winning by a nose. It's that extra something - energy, time, discipline or focus - that someone is willing to put in, that turns the tide and transforms the outcome.

Growing In The Direction
Of Your Dreams

I believe that many people want to go to another level - but not everyone seizes the opportunity to reach their peak performance. Unfortunately, most of us settle into a comfort zone where we rarely challenge ourselves. We stop asking the questions we need to ask, to allow us to advance to another level.

The most successful areas of our lives often just need a small tweak to be remarkable. Like polishing dull silver to a brilliant luster, ordinary families can outshine the status quo and become extraordinary families if they're willing to invest a little more awareness where it counts. A plateaued business can become a high-performance business. Ordinary teams can become exemplary ones. By optimizing our strengths, we can take many areas of our lives to the next level.

George Washington Carver saw potential the size of a peanut and transformed an entire industry. An agricultural chemist and brilliant inventor, he made it his mission to find over 300 uses of the peanut ranging from shave cream to synthetic rubber. His inventions revolutionized the economics of farming in the late 1800s, guaranteeing that the world would never see the peanut the same way. "When you do the common things in life in an uncommon way, you will command the attention of the world," he once said of his discoveries. If Carver could do so much with so little, just think what peanut-sized potential lies within you if you will dare to discover it.

If you don't ever challenge yourself, you will never uncover your full potential. As a young man in high school, I recall telling my mom that I would one day have a certain house, a certain car and a certain lifestyle that could make these things a reality. My mom loved me, but she did not want me to set myself up for disappointment. I took that to mean that she didn't believe I could do it. The challenge she set before me was a huge motivational factor for me to decide that I would do whatever it took to do exactly what I envisioned myself doing as a senior in high school. Whatever you deem success to be—being a great wife, a great father or a great business person—when you challenge yourself to follow that plan, I think the outcome will always take care of itself.

John F. Kennedy defined happiness this way: "The full use of your powers along lines of excellence." Applying every last measure of your strength, talent, focus and energy toward excellence in the areas that are most important to you will bring you happiness and fulfillment like you've never known.

What amazes me is the amount of time we have on our hands to get better in any area of our lives. Using drive time to and from the office or carpool, we have the opportunity to listen to a book on tape. We can call our mentor with some life questions during our commute. We can read a book in the evenings. If you're learning something all the time, you are growing in the direction of your dreams.

Starting out as an independent agent, I was fired up to learn everything I could. I started reading motivational books and anything that taught me the art of being. Before long, I had found a mentor and met several peers with similar goals. We discussed our goals and consistently motivated each other. I invested in the wisdom of those who had gone before me. I was already focused on reaching peak performance in every area of my life, and now I had people helping me along.

Did it take extra time out of my day? Yes. Did it require additional effort and energy? Certainly. We rarely feel the thrill of dreaming a little bigger, applying extra energy toward a greater goal and winning by a nose unless we sacrifice. However, when we step outside of the box to tackle something difficult and have the courage to believe that we can do it, we begin building momentum. I can't think of anything more frustrating than missing the life you always wanted to live by a nose.

IT'S ALL IN THE APPROACH

That we continually improve our lives is crucial. How we do it, makes or breaks our ability to improve and reach our fullest potential. Improving doesn't mean focusing on what's wrong and fixing it. In fact, just the opposite works best. Possibility-thinkers start by focusing on what's right in their lives, businesses, homes and communities and then figure out how to improve it.

It doesn't take any special skills to point out what's wrong with someone or something else. However, it takes a passion for possibility to create a habit of identifying what's going well in a family, in a business, in a relationship or in a community and then consistently seeking ways to ramp it up. Possibility-thinkers are never satisfied with status quo. "Good enough" is the enemy of what's best in our personal lives, jobs and relationships. "Good enough" is just arriving at a place where life doesn't hurt. "Good enough" is the stepsister of "fantastic and amazing." "Good enough" is a survivor, not a thriver. Unfortunately, these days we even hand out trophies and awards for "good enough."

In February 2008, the Seattle-based coffee giant Starbucks surprised the business world (and many of its customers) by closing close to seven thousand of its U.S. locations for a day to hold an intensive three-hour training session for its baristas. The chief executive of Starbucks said on the company website that the point of the nationwide closure was to "teach, educate and share our love of coffee and the art of espresso" with its employees.

That is possibility-thinking in action.

Was something drastically wrong with the company that they had to hold this training? No. In fact, it was just the opposite. They decided to improve on a good thing while things were going well.

This is totally contrary to our natural way of thinking. When we are ready to improve areas in our lives, what do we naturally want to do? We focus on what's wrong and try to fix it! If it's our business, we focus on the less productive employee. If it's our family, we focus on the rebellious child's habits.

Have you heard the phrase, "Love is blind?" We often hear the phrase in the context of relationships between men and women who are so in love that they look past each other's odd quirks and flaws. That's true love. Love does not focus on weaknesses and mistakes and try to fix it - it focuses on strengths and beauty.

I Love You. You're Perfect.
Now Change.

There was a popular Broadway play with the humorous title, *I Love You. You're Perfect. Now Change.* Have you ever noticed how often we try to change the people we love? Here's an example: a woman falls in love with a charming guy who has an outgoing personality and many friends. She loves the way he handles a crowd and how he welcomes new people into the group as if they were long lost friends.

Fast-forward 10 months when the couple is standing at the altar getting married and a few more months after that. They're spending every moment together, eating dinner at home and renting movies to watch on the weekends. He's growing restless to be with the gang, and her feelings are hurt because she wonders why he doesn't want to spend all his time with her.

He's happy to stay at home and read books together on the couch in order to avoid a confrontation, but that isn't the guy she married. Whether she realizes it or not, she's trying to change his core personality.

Suddenly, love has its eyes wide open. It's no longer blind to certain faults. If this couple in our example isn't careful, their relationship will soon be headed in the wrong direction.

I have found that the principle "love is blind" applies in a much greater context inside of our offices, community groups, churches, schools—anywhere you find people in relationships with each other. Your time will be used much more efficiently if you spend it honing someone's strengths instead of trying to fix their weaknesses.

A recent Gallup poll revealed that most unhappy employees quit because of their managers, not necessarily because they didn't like their jobs or the company. As Marcus Buckingham notes in his book, *First Break All the Rules,* too many managers spend too much time trying to correct someone's weakness, rather than focusing on their strengths.

But what do we do with the weaknesses in the meantime? (And by weakness, I mean anything that differs from what we expect another person to be or do.)

OVERLOOK It

One way of dealing with a person's weakness is to overlook it altogether. Most personality assessment tests teach that every personality strength has an underlying weakness. Those we associate as strong, leader-type Lions can bite people's heads off, and the Beavers who like to get things done can work themselves to death. Every personality profile has its accompanying weakness. You'll find it if you look hard enough. Why go looking for the weakness?

REFRAME It

Another way of dealing with someone's weakness is to reframe it. At work, the way a leader sees a particular weakness controls its impact on the individual and his or her job performance. You can empower a weakness by fixating on it so much that you begin to associate the individual with the weakness. You may say, "That Sally - she's not a math person."

51

Maybe that's true about Sally, but why not capitalize on her strengths instead? "That Sally—she's a genius at organizing things."

DELEGATE It

A third way to deal with someone's weaknesses is something we discussed in an earlier chapter—learn to delegate it. Delegate what people are not good at doing so that they are free to pursue what they are good at doing. This will do wonders for their self-esteem and save you a lot of headaches.

It's insane to continue to ask someone to play to their weaknesses and expect a good result. All that does is slow productivity and weaken the person concerned. A better way is to delegate that obstacle and help them discover *what else* they are really good at doing.

FINDING OUT WHAT SOMEONE LOVES TO DO

When you ask people to tell you about their passions, several things happen. First, you honor them by simply being interested in who they are. Second, you get to see what makes them light up. Third, you get to share and profit from the very best they have to offer. Displaying personal interest in your employees and family inspires loyalty.

You can see this principle at work in families. Parents may mean well when they sign up a child for piano lessons. However, what if the child really doesn't like the piano but comes to life on the basketball court? Which activity do you think will be easier to get the child to practice at home - piano or basketball? Sometimes we make it difficult on ourselves by not listening to what lights people up.

Passion is an inside job. Trying to force, cajole or encourage someone to develop passion about an activity or job responsibility that he or she really doesn't like will never work. Work with their God-given talents and abilities instead.

Even knowing what a person *hates to do* can be very revealing. I always ask a potential employee, "What do you *love* to do and what do you *hate* to do? What do you want to do more of in your job and what do you want to do less of?" When people simply tolerate the things about their job that they really don't enjoy doing, morale declines and productivity sinks.

By contrast, when you love what you're doing, work is play and you're naturally passionate about it. Productivity soars when we're having fun and doing what we do best. People wind up being mediocre in life for two reasons. One, they're so busy trying to address their weaknesses that they forget to grow their strengths; or two, they're trying to fit into the boss/ parent/partner's vision for their lives. People aligned with passion see their jobs as an opportunity to play and grow at the same time. I think the most miserable thing anybody could do is to take something as precious as life and live it without enjoyment.

We all have untapped potential. Remember to ask yourself constantly, "What do I love to do?" This voyage of 'self-uncovery' may take you to some amazing adventures in your life.

Seeing Individuals, Not Job Descriptions

I also see the principle of "love is blind" playing out in the business world in the way business leaders hire people and build job descriptions around them. A good leader recognizes the individuals behind the job titles or roles in the office. Instead of seeing five accountants, a receptionist and one assistant in the office, a good leader does the math and sees seven individuals, with seven different strengths, all working for one team.

Job descriptions are stagnant, black-and-white descriptions on paper. They have no depth. Individuals grow. Their job descriptions should grow with them, allowing them to shed the responsibilities they have outgrown and find new challenges that are just a little bigger than they are.

Although it's human nature to want to focus on what we do, that's not what makes us who we are. To have a team of highly motivated individuals, you must allow for independent thinkers. You may think you have your team's potential all figured out - but if you focus on them as individuals they will always surprise you by doing even more than they thought they could do.

Getting The Right Players In The Right Positions On The Team

Every professional sports team uses systems in one of two ways to utilize the talents on their team. Some coaches apply the system to the talent; others apply the talent to the system. However, if you don't have a system to fit your talent, it won't work. And if you don't have the right kind of talent to fit your system, it won't work either.

I remember a time when a sales assistant and a service assistant both worked in my office. They were recent hires, about two or three months into their roles. Although both people were capable of functioning in either role, I could see that their productivity level was not what it could be in either case. They enjoyed the work, but they weren't playing to their strengths. One day I asked them what they liked and disliked about their roles.

Their answers revealed their true gifts and showed me exactly what needed to happen. We flip-flopped their jobs.

The sales assistant went into the service department, and the service assistant stepped right into the sales role. We wrote job descriptions around each one's aptitudes that would add value to the company and set them free from their old responsibilities. The result was two happy team players whose productivity soared within days of starting their new jobs.

In his book *Good to Great*, Jim Collins writes about having the right people on the "bus" (the analogy he uses for a team or company), but they're sitting in the wrong seats. You don't want to kick them off the bus, but something needs to change. Once you get the right people into the right positions they should play on the team, everything starts to click. New possibilities unfold.

PEOPLE HAVE TO WANT TO CHANGE

We are not in a position to optimize other people's roles in our business or at home if they don't want to change. All the road maps to success, goal-setting and mentoring are useless unless the team players want to change.

Why is that? Simple. When we try to change others, they often think we're saying in essence, *"I don't like something about who you are."*

One of the most important lessons about winning by a nose and reaching the next level in life is to realize the importance of *wanting to change.*

People who are frightened of change will perceive your well-intentioned observations as a personal attack. It's not your job to change others. Only they can do that.

Success is based on what needs changing, not who needs changing. Ask yourself, *"What* about this situation needs changing?" In the context of someone's strengths, change is acceptable if it means to simply improve or mature an area where someone already has a natural affinity or talent and take it to the next level.

CHARACTER IS THE ANTIDOTE TO WEAKNESS

It's similar to performing the work of a blacksmith. A piece of steel goes through a change process called tempering. A blacksmith builds strength upon strength in a piece of steel by placing it into an intense flame, pulling it out and hammering it until it cools. This process doesn't eliminate weaknesses in the steel; it builds layer upon layer of strength in the metal until it is equal to the task for which it is required.

That's what it means to develop one's character. *Character is not what is left over once you have eliminated all of your weaknesses.* In fact, increasing strengths ultimately allows for the weakness to become redundant and fall away. If you attempt to eliminate your weaknesses without working on your strengths, all you will have at the end is a broken spirit and a defeated mindset.

Character is the culmination of the strengths built into our lives that determine our responses regardless of the situation. It develops over time, and it needs to be constantly refined. When character is developed consciously, it becomes the antidote to weakness. I've found that when I focus on honing our personal strengths, the weaknesses often take care of themselves.

Consider a child who brings home a report card to mom and dad. The report has straight A's, except for a C in chemistry. What gets the parents' attention first? Unfortunately, the temptation is to forfeit the opportunity to praise the child for the outstanding work in the other subjects in favor of pointing out the lower grade.

Try obsessing over the A's and see what happens. Nourish the child's character by praising his or her diligence and hard work. Affirm the personal discipline and strength of character he or she showed in earning such good grades. Children soak up personal praise, especially from their parents, like a sponge. See if the C's start turning into B's over time and possibly even A's. The weakness will have taken care of itself.

CULTIVATING CHARACTER

Have you ever noticed how much emphasis is placed on *doing* all the right things so that you can have the life you want? We're bombarded with new and improved ways of *doing* things in our jobs, relationships and personal lives that will produce success. However, there is far too little formal training on how to become a better person. Everything starts with the building blocks inside of us called character. Sometimes the most difficult place to start believing we can make a change is within ourselves. Encouraging ourselves to become the people we want to be will motivate us to live life on purpose and constantly pursue possibilities and opportunities.

CHAPTER Five

BECOMING THE PERSON YOU DREAMED YOU COULD BE

My father left school in the sixth grade. He moved from Puerto Rico to New York City. All by himself. He always hated it when people realized he was a deaf mute and equated that with being dumb. There was nothing stupid about my father. He had a business education from the school of life, and he made the most of it.

My mother is French-Irish - a kind and loving woman who has never told a lie her entire life. She moves through life with grace. She met my father at a deaf bowling event when they were very young and they married soon after. I was born in Manhattan near West 47th Street when my mom was only seventeen.

Two deaf mutes having a baby at a young age presented some challenges. I once asked my mother how she knew when I was crying. She just put me sideways in bed with her at night. "When you cried," she told me, "you would kick my belly and that was how I knew when to take care of you." My parents were the first to teach me that anything was possible because they lived it every day of their lives adjusting to a hearing world.

They took it all in stride. My father loved people and had a great sense of humor. It seems he was always laughing and making others laugh, too. He had a paint and body shop where he built a sterling reputation for being the best in the business. I guess losing his sense of hearing sharpened all his other senses. He could turn out more beautifully restored cars than any other body shop "artist" in town.

My maternal grandfather was the superintendent of our building. He lived on the first floor and was responsible for the eight tenants in the four-story building. Since my parents were both born deaf, my grandparents taught me how to talk. I began interpreting in sign language for my parents when I was only five or six years old.

Their dependence on my access to a hearing world created a tight bond at an early age that wasn't always comfortable for me. I always felt as if people were staring at me when I signed with my parents in a grocery store or in a mall. Like most teens, I didn't want to be different from my peers or stand out from the crowd. Looking back, I see I had the usual angst of "parental embarrassment"—times two because mine had a unique challenge that made them different from the other parents at school.

What I didn't realize then was that they were arming me with the gifts of a communicator. Looking them in the eyes when I spoke and being clear about what I needed to say showed me that differences are often strengths in disguise. But try telling that to a sixth grader.

Don't worry, just be

I was attending my sixth grade parent-teacher meeting, filled with my classmates and their parents and, of course, mine. As the teacher outlined the upcoming events for the school year, I began to grow nervous. I was extremely self-conscious and didn't want all the other kids to watch me relay the information to my parents in sign language.

Mom and Dad kept nudging me and signing, "What is the teacher saying?" My plan was to sit quietly, listen well and tell them about it later.

"Stop asking me what they are saying," I signed back sharply, trying to pretend that we weren't different. "I'll tell you later."

I was just trying to act cool because I desperately wanted to be like everyone else. My parents were less than impressed. The more I tried to hush them up, the more forceful their signing became. "What is the teacher saying, Son!?" they signed with a flurry of motions.

A hush in the classroom drew my attention to the fact that the class had ceased listening to the teacher and all eyes were on me instead. I was square in the spotlight. Precisely where I did not want to be with everyone staring at the three of us. I wished the ground would open up around me and just swallow me up. My father saw how embarrassed I was. He looked straight at me with pain in his eyes and signed, "Stop worrying about what everyone else thinks. Just be."

At that same moment, my teacher figured out she had lost the attention of the class. Not realizing my parents were deaf mutes, she saw me using my hands and said, "Jose, would you like to share something with the class?" clearly irritated at the distraction I was causing.

"Mrs. Horn," I began sheepishly, "My parents were just asking me what you are saying. But I didn't want to interrupt the class."

That really upset my dad. He signed again with a flourish, "Son, don't worry about what other people think. Just be!"

A few years later when I was 15, we attended a sports banquet and my coach stood up to give a speech. As he began, my parents turned to me to interpret for them.

Again, I didn't want to draw attention to myself. So, I just smiled as if I were intently interested in the speaker and overlooked their insistence. Out of the corner of my eye, I once more saw my father sign, "Don't worry about other people. Just be, Son."

There was that stupid sentence again and I still did not understand what he was saying.

Me as fraternity president? no way José

During the first or second week of classes in my freshman year of college I joined a fraternity. I met a fellow student at Montgomery Wards where I was working 30 hours a week selling appliances to pay for school.

He invited me to a couple of rush parties. I went through pledging and noticed that they were doing a lot of unnecessary things in the process. However, since I was only a freshman, I just went through everything else with all the other guys.

I have always enjoyed helping people to have a good time. Because I had to translate for my parents from such an early age, I became very sensitive to the needs of the people around me. When I noticed people standing by themselves at a party at a fraternity function, I would go over to them and make them feel included and welcome. I served as chairman of several social functions. Always the planner, I came up with a couple of new systems for rushing quality people. I even made the parties a lot nicer. The turning point came when I was encouraged to run for president of the fraternity.

On the one hand, we had me, the guy who drove a $600 Chevy Impala and worked at Montgomery wards 30 hours a week. I lived in a little one bedroom apartment. I was paying my own way through college, guardian of my little brother and sister and having to interpret for my deaf parents. And I was dead broke.

And then there was Troy. Troy fit the mold of a fraternity president to a "T." He was from a wealthy family enjoying a free ride to college, living in a luxury two-bedroom apartment. The guy had a beautiful 280ZX and came from Highland Park in Dallas.

I never thought of myself as a president of anything. So there was Troy and I hanging out outside waiting for the results of the vote (and I knew what that was going to be). It wasn't long in coming. As we stood there, I had my game face on and my congratulatory handshake ready.

When they announced José Feliciano as President of the 1982 Sigma Phi Epsilon fraternity, I sat down on the nearest chair with a bump. The world went quiet for just a few seconds, and I don't remember hearing much around me. That's when it hit me. I finally got what my father had been trying to teach me all those years ago. *Stop worrying about what everyone else thinks.* **Just be!** *Don't try to be someone else!*

It turns out that the same parents that I was embarrassed about because they were different, were the same people who'd taught me the most powerful lesson in my life. *Just be!* I had friendship, love, family and health. They'd taught me to be aware, caring and considerate, and they'd grown a leader.

For the first time in my life, I was just being me and not worrying about what others thought. And the feeling was overwhelming: absolutely right, humbling and strangely good.

WHAT'S INSIDE MATTERS MOST

I could feel my perspective beginning to change, as "aha" after "aha" sunk in. "Just be" was the reason I had won. "Just be" was the reason that I had friends and family who loved me. Those two words became the foundation of my character.

It's not what you have or don't have that matters most; it's who you are. Once you get that, everything you want has permission to line up and fall into place.

I realized the importance of "just be" just in time. By the time I was 18, my parents had divorced and my mom named me the legal guardian of my siblings. I soon became aware of the fact that three little pairs of eyes and ears were paying close attention to everything their older brother did or said. Up to that point, I'd spent most of my life being uncomfortable with and even ashamed of my parents' differences. I knew I didn't want my siblings growing up that way. Because I changed my attitude toward my parents at just the right time, my siblings never perceived them as different or less capable.

Be, do and have. in that order!

Before you can do and have all that you imagine in life, you have to "be" first. You have to be willing to cultivate a strong character. Anytime you can do anything to become a better you, it has tremendous results. A lot of times, we approach a relationship with the idea of, "What's in it for me?" The question should be, "How can I add value here?" Good investments equal strong returns. That's true with everything that you do in life. Financial investments require money carefully invested; character investments require investments of your second primary currency: time. There is always room to *become* a better person who *does* greater things. *In that order.* You have to be the person you most want to be first in order for you to do what needs doing so that you can have what you most want to have. Be, do, have.

I think we get it backwards. Many times. I hear people say, "Boy, if I had this (material item), I could be anyone I wanted to be." But that's not necessarily true. Modern advertising makes us feel as though we would be different people who are happier and more successful if we only had a certain product. The products are the perks, not the requirement.

Sure, some people are drawn to a successful person because of what he or she may have, but it's the being part that keeps them there. A person's character can make you think that maybe if you hang around them for a bit, whatever they have inside may just rub off on you, too. Knowing how to "just be" is crucial to success. That's why you have to "live it" before you can do it or have it.

Clarity of "being" comes next. If a mom says, "My goal is to raise good children and be a great wife," she is successful if she achieves that, no matter what she has or doesn't have. You are the one who gets to define your success. It's important that the picture in your mind and the feeling inside of you matches up with what is in front of you.

Success for my wife means being a great wife and mother. And she's constantly focused on it and challenging herself in the area of personal growth. I believe that the hunger and pursuit of excellence in our lives is missing for too many of us, and yet it's the treasure map that leads to real fulfillment.

Business people forget that they are selling themselves, not their product. That comes second. Realtors do not sell houses; they sell themselves. Pharmaceutical reps don't sell medicines; they sell themselves. Whether it's our personal values, ideas, politics, worldviews, religion - whatever the case may be - who we are matters more and makes a longer-lasting impression to people than what we do.

You Are Your Most Valuable Asset

It strikes me that we are careful to pass wealth and material goods from generation to generation, but equally careless when it comes to passing on family values to our children. If all they inherit is the money, they miss out on the real treasure—the character behind the story of how the wealth was accumulated. The real deal behind the success. Without that story, the money is incomplete, looking for a place to anchor. It's the story that creates a dynasty, a sense of respect for the characters who created incredible wealth and accumulated amazing stories of courage and perseverance along the way. Money is the byproduct; the story is the wealth.

Many successful people fail four or five times before they hit their stride. The patriarch of a family may be a wealthy man today, but what people don't realize is that he may have won and lost a fortune two or three times before he got there.

The grandchildren think granddad always had it big. So, they don't learn to participate in the adventure he has begun and add their own unique next chapter. They don't look at the man behind the money. All they see is the good life. Unless they add an episode or two of their own, they'll never be able to fully appreciate the fruits of his labor or make sure the next crop is ready for harvest. Worse yet, they may fail to inherit his strength and character along with the money. That's like having the pie with no filling.

You may have heard the saying that once you've become a millionaire it is easy to become a millionaire again. There's some truth to that. After the first million, the millionaire has a map for what's required. He understands the rules. And the equipment he needs, including the character he has so carefully cultivated, is all in place. Now, all he has to do is duplicate the pattern. Who he became along the way is now worth many more millions of dollars. It might be a long journey to that second million. However, this time, he's ready.

When people inherit money from the previous generation without the accompanying work ethic or the desire to succeed, (the real wealth) statistics show that the wealth has evaporated by the third generation.

In fact, today's statistics reveal that 90% of all inheritances are gone within 18 months.

Why is that? The money is passed on, but not the values. What we haven't earned (or will not nurture), we have little chance of keeping. Therefore, communicating the family mission statement - a vision statement of the family that everybody could buy into - is something that we should all be doing from the day our children are old enough to hear it. If we set expectations for their part in it and look at positioning their strengths within the family business, we can confidently expect the next generation to run an organization after we have gone. We have to make sure they learn to develop those leadership skills and character qualities that brought success in the first place. That's our responsibility. It's part of a growing a successful society which is, after all, an extension of our business.

I created an interview process with my clients to walk people through the life lessons they've learned along the way. The response has been phenomenal as people get a chance to help their kids inherit so much more than just dollars and cents. They want their descendants to know the family story and understand the family values. They want them to know what their great-grandfather was thinking when he had money. And when he lost money, how did that affect him and how did he make it back?

We develop character throughout our lives, but the process begins in our families. It starts from the time we are small and lasts forever as we gain more and more experience. In my own family, I can pinpoint different experiences where my parents took the opportunity to shape my character.

CHALLENGES DEVELOP
CHARACTER

I remember the drive to the water department. I was only nine at the time, but I recall rehearsing in my mind exactly what I would say to the people in the office when we got there. My family had just moved to Atlanta, Georgia from Manhattan. I had never seen so many green grassy areas or such open spaces in my life.

I am a native New Yorker, but when I was growing up, the city was a very different place. Back then, I walked a few blocks from where my family lived to public school #51 every day in the third grade. Now we were starting over again in a new city, in a completely different part of the country where they spoke much more slowly and said things like "Ya'll."

As the oldest son, I had to help make some of the arrangements for our family's cross-country move from New York to the South. And on this day, our first day in Atlanta, we needed to arrange to have the electricity and utilities turned on so we could move in.

I understood how money worked because my parents would explain it to me using the checkbook registry. I talked with my parents about what needed to happen to establish services where we would live. As we walked into the water department that day, I'm sure it surprised the lady behind the front counter when she asked my parents, "How may I help you?" and my parents both turned to look at me. I learned to handle adult situations from an early age.

Growing Up Different
Is A Blessing

I received the gift of parents who, in their own way, expected me to be a leader at every opportunity and gave me ample circumstances to apply what I was learning. By the time I was 18, I had a full handle on the activities involved in daily family living. It created a lot of trust in our family and built my self-confidence. I knew more about family responsibilities than most students much older than me.

Sadly, many families don't involve their kids in the day-to-day operations of a family, and that perpetuates ignorance and builds a lack of trust. It seems to me that part of the reason that some parents don't have a lot of confidence in the way their kids handle money is that they didn't allow their children to be involved in the financial process growing up. Consequently, they never developed the mindset and skills necessary to understand the value and role of money in the family. Isn't it funny how we sometimes unintentionally help create the very scenarios we most wanted to avoid?

As I lead families through financial and life planning, I've noticed that parents who are very open with their children tend to be much closer emotionally. There seems to be a lot more trust between members of the family. Oftentimes in families like these, the assets stand a better chance of surviving from generation to generation because parents have taken the time to teach the children about value and the way money works. The kids also know the story behind the wealth. They inherit it all.

On the other hand, there are parents who don't trust their kids to handle the family finances. These parents often don't realize how they contributed long ago to the adult children's inability to function in a world of finance, relationships and personal values. The stalemate in communication permeates the family. The adult children are directionless because they were never included in the map-making process.

No one develops character in a vacuum. It's amazing how much we contribute to developing each other's character - enhancing it or depleting it - by some of the little things we do or don't do.

I don't think my parents have ever fully understood that they were doing me a favor by involving me in family responsibilities that many people would have considered too much for a child to handle. When you're deaf coming into a hearing world, there is a lot more you have to do to simply survive. I watched my deaf parents do better than survive. They raised a family and taught me that anyone could make it.

Praising Someone's Character
Every Chance You Get

Does character matter if you get the job done? To me, it's the only way to get the job done. It matters in everything that you do. It requires that you evaluate your own life and lead by example. Character raises the standard everywhere. It's often underrated yet crucial to lasting success.

Sadly, we don't recognize it enough in our homes, offices and communities. We forget to acknowledge positive character traits in other people, instead of citing their shortcomings.

It is one thing to see strength of character in an individual and another to recognize it. We may observe compassion and dependability in others. However, we seldom go the extra mile and acknowledge or honor the quality we observe.

We are so caught up in recognizing accomplishments that we forget to acknowledge quality and character strengths. For example, we could say to someone, "Thanks for getting those notes to me before my meeting." That is recognizing what someone did to contribute to a smooth office environment. And it is important. However, I would rather say to the person who brought me the notes, "Your dependability allows this team to function well. I'm grateful that I'm able to rely on you."

It's the difference between showing gratitude for what people *do* and expressing appreciation for *who* they are. Showing gratitude is almost compulsory and can be accomplished by a simple "thank you." And yet I'm guessing that we probably don't even practice this simple step enough. We don't write enough thank you notes. We overlook making that extra phone call to tell someone that we're grateful. When we express sincere appreciation, we go beyond what they do for us and touch on *who they are*. Where gratitude is generally thankful, appreciation truly validates.

Of course, recognition that takes place in front of others amplifies the effect. People stand taller. They want to do more, and they certainly want to be around someone who values both their contribution and them as

67

people. I try to do that in my office, and I can see the amazing impact that it makes on our team.

WE NEED EACH OTHER

Once I mastered the wisdom behind my father's philosophy - just be - I came to another life-changing realization. As a result of beginning to love and accept who I was, I began to find it even easier to love and accept others without them having to do things to make it happen.

The truth is that we need other people in order to allow us to fulfill our life goals. They're your leverage; you simply can't maximize your potential without them. You have a part you must play, but you have to allow others to play their part, too. Possibility - thinking opens the door to many opportunities that require teamwork. If you want to maximize your success, you are going to need to partner with other people. And then it's all about all of you. When you begin to do truly great things, it can no longer just be about you. That's gold in the bank. There's no limit to what you can accomplish in life. Together.

CHAPTER Six

PARTNERING WITH PEOPLE AND BUILDING THE IMPOSSIBLE

B aseball is one of my passions, and I was heartbroken when I found out that my city planned to demolish an historic ballpark and turn it into a parking lot. The stadium, boasting a seating capacity of 4,000 was unusual for Tyler in the 1940's. Back then Tyler was just a little East Texas town outside the Big D, Dallas. Still, it had been the home of several professional, semi-professional and collegiate baseball teams dating all the way back to 1941.

I began to follow the efforts to save this historic stadium with interest. Some city leaders petitioned the Tyler city council for $25,000 to make much needed renovations. They were summarily turned down.

I happened to be at that meeting and afterwards I asked the petitioner what all needed to be done to the park to bring it back to life. He rattled off a list that included major projects like painting the walls and repairing the dugout and stadium seats. That night I could not stop thinking about how much our community would lose by destroying such an important part of East Texas history. I decided I would at least push it a little further to see if there was any hope of restoring it to its former glory.

By the following morning, I couldn't stand it any longer. I went out to Hightower Lumber Company by myself and met with a gentleman who agreed to accompany me to the ballpark to see the project for himself.

When we arrived, we parked on an old blacktop full of potholes that served as a parking lot and we walked onto the field. A couple of stray cats darted out from the dugouts and the wind whipped up the dirt and weeds growing freely on the pitcher's mound. It was hard to even imagine a day when these broken metal seats had held thousands of cheering fans rooting for the home team.

We made quite a pair that day—he in his coveralls and me in my business suit. We turned our attention first to the dugouts that were now warped and worn. It looked bad—almost hopeless. Nevertheless, I tried to stay positive and asked, "So, what kind of lumber do we need to build out these dugouts?"

To make matters worse, he and I both knew that there wasn't a budget for any of this because the plans to demolish it had been in the newspaper for quite some time. So, in exchange for his lumber and labor, I made him an offer that I was sure he couldn't refuse. I proudly told him I would give the lumber company a 19 x 14 ad on the outfield wall once we were up and running again.

He smiled politely and just kicked up some dirt with the toe of his boot. Squinting in the morning sun, he put his hands in his pockets and said slowly, "Son, I don't really want an ad out on the wall."

I was devastated. Looking back, he must have thought I was absolutely out of my mind to even dream of restoring this old park. *What kind of lumber would it take?* Not free lumber, anyway. He knew I didn't have any money for this, so that didn't really leave me much to barter with.

"Sure, I understand," I began. "I'm sorry that I wasted your time."

"I don't really want an ad on the wall," he repeated. "But I want to help you if I can. I've always had a dream for what this field could be."

The next day, several trucks from his company rumbled onto the blacktop and dropped off load after load of prime lumber in front of the dugouts. The dream had begun to take shape.

I had a fraternity brother at the time who was in the construction business, and it just so happened that he knew how to set and build the dugouts. Within a matter of days, we had permission from the city to begin construction. A whole crew of volunteers came with their sleeves rolled up and their hard hats on. Our first task was sanding the old paint off the outfield fence to prepare it for a fresh coat. As I sanded off those huge flakes of dried paint and dirt, I smiled imagining all the home runs that had soared over that fence the past sixty years. And it looked like the home runs would keep on flying.

Before the project was over, I had convinced several other local companies and individuals to buy a few of the 9 x 14 signs on the fence to help us out. Finally when the facelift was completed with new stadium seats, new dugouts and a renewed field, we had spent less than $900. In other words, when we volunteered and teamed up with other partners we had accomplished the same project that had been estimated to cost $25,000! There is no way to underestimate the value of good partnerships.

I learned a valuable lesson through this experience: *it's better to work together than it is to work alone.* People are willing to participate in your dreams if you let them. There is something inside each of us that longs to attempt the impossible and make a difference.

If you show people a dream and explain the value of their part and *how* they can make a difference, they will usually sign up pretty fast. They simply need to see beyond the *cost* of their commitment to the *impact* that they can make. When there is a noble endeavor involved, most partners won't ask for anything in return. Our world is full of people just waiting to be asked to be a part of something incredible.

PRINCIPLES FOR
PARTNERING WITH OTHERS

Teamwork is one of the most powerful forces in our world. It impacts every area of our lives. When I coached little league football, the parents would often pull me aside after practice and say things like, "Coach, I want to thank you. This football team is more than just a sport for my son. It has given him direction and structure in his life for the first time. Now he has dreams."

My kids were all from an underprivileged neighborhood, and what they learned on the field spilled over into their everyday lives. I'll never forget how proud (and shocked) the mothers were when they told me their sons actually cleaned their rooms now and helped around the house with chores. They were doing better in school and making more positive choices.

I often think that God must have wanted us to work as teams because He put us in families right away. No baby is born all alone. There are no Lone Rangers in the hospital nursery! (And even he had Tonto.) From the moment we're born, we depend on others to help us learn to live life to its fullest. Why do we think we should make it alone when we're older? There are several principles I've learned about partnering with other people to achieve more in life.

Learning To Care For Each Other

Football is fun, and it's good for physical development, but it's also where my players learned the value of teamwork. They weren't just a bunch of individuals out on a field when we worked and played together - they were part of a team. Each player needed the other to succeed. When one person scored, the whole team benefited. We shared all the ups and all the downs and found out each team member had the potential to affect another for the better.

There were times when some of my players felt like quitting. They thought the game was too hard, or they were frustrated by their lack of progress. It made me proud when I saw the other kids encouraging them in their own childlike ways to keep going.

We all have to learn to trust each other during rough times in our lives. It works the same way on a little league football team as it does in a family of four or a Fortune 500 organization.

I've also discovered the value of this principle as a husband. I have learned how important it is for me to trust my wife when she makes a decision related to our child. It's one way I can show her that we are on the same team. We once took a parenting class called, *Growing Kids God's Way.* We learned that the unity of a mother and father affects a child. Communicating that unity to our daughter makes her feel safe. There are no sides for her to choose.

A child becomes an extension of the bond between his or her parents. Supporting and caring for one another means we are winning together as a family.

Finding Out What's Important To Others

One of my co-workers was struggling with unmanageable debt. She had tried unsuccessfully to sell her house, and the situation was suffocating her. We sat down to consider her options. Together, we began to map the way out of debt and into dreams. By the time we finished, she was breathing a whole lot easier, and there was even a hint of a smile.

This co-worker implemented her plan with enthusiasm, and I saw something incredible happen over the next two months. Making positive decisions in her financial life affected her on an emotional level, and that spilled over to an improved attitude about her work. Instead of being depressed, she began to show tremendous pride in her work. I learned I could depend on her completely, and she became an extremely loyal employee.

Helping people gain clarity about their goals is the key to partnering. When you help others grow, your own growth is inevitable. Mapping out the things that are important to them - and showing them ways they can implement the steps necessary to reach their fullest potential - is one of the most fulfilling parts of my life.

I realized a long time ago that none of my employees are forced to work for me. They can work anywhere they choose. In reality, they are working for themselves, through my business, to attain their own goals, dreams and desires. If I can help them develop a game plan to achieve their goals, chances are they will return the favor by helping me to achieve mine.

I treat my customers, vendors and employees the same way. I partner with each of them for the best results, for all of us.

Of course, you'll always find people who have little or no self-motivation. For them, making a paycheck to pay their bills is the big picture. These are some of my favorite people. I love to watch the look on there faces the first time they discover there is a big goal out there with their name on it. My reward is showing them how to move from the only picture they know to a much larger one.

Communicating The Game Plan

Another principle for partnering with others requires that the game plan be clear to everyone on the team. Every successful team understands the overall game plan. Some businesses call it a mission statement. I don't just limit it to the workplace. Even our family has their own mission statement. It describes our values and defines where we're going.

Many poorly run organizations are filled with people who are clueless about the team's game plan. They haven't a clue about the specific role that they should play. It's like the story I heard about two men who were struggling to get a bulky piece of furniture through a narrow door. They were grunting and groaning to make it fit. One man said, "We almost have it in." At that point, the guy on the other end said, "*In*? I thought we were trying to get it *out*!" A leader's challenge is to communicate clearly the overall game plan in any endeavor.

Assigning Roles On The Team

Getting people into the right places in an organization is crucial. That means breaking down the game plan for success into different parts and seeing which role fits each player.

On my little league team, there were all kinds of positions for the kids to play. When we started each season, everyone wanted to be the quarterback, but a team can't function with eleven quarterbacks on the field. My job was to communicate the importance of each position. Once that was achieved, everything just came together.

You can always tell when your team "gets it" and understands their role in the big game plan. Once the roles and expectations are clear, and everyone respects each other, it creates a high-performance team in a positive, creative environment. When this happens, your team is unstoppable and anything becomes possible!

Recognizing Contributions To The Team

Everyone enjoys recognition for a job well done. As a coach, one of my most important jobs was recognizing my kids' strengths and weaknesses and then playing to their strengths. A successful team is a band of successful individuals, each working in their strengths.

We all have the same goal - to participate in winning the game. Recognizing individual accomplishments encourages everyone to constantly search for and deliver their personal best. Recognizing contributions to the success of the overall game makes people work harder together.

Realizing It's Easier To Work Together Instead Of Alone

Coming from a tight knit family who overcame difficult odds and now works together in the same business, we've all realized that *it's easier to work together than it is to work apart.*

Many brothers and sisters have just the opposite experience. They don't get along well or even talk to each other. However, our experiences have grown us closer together. We approach every opportunity with positive expectations. And we just go from there - together.

Those who try to work alone seldom reach their full potential. Masterminding is simply creating a third mind when two people come up with several good ideas that lead to even greater ones. There is always somebody else in your office, in your neighborhood, in your class, etc. who wants to achieve the same goals as you.

I remember as a kid, running from house to house looking for someone to come out and play. Sometimes we built forts, and sometimes we got splinters in our fingers trying to put together a rickety old tree house. Whatever we did, we were just out there playing together. That's the same way I feel about work.

If you approach work that way, the pressure is off. Misery comes when we grumble about our job. However, once you look at it as playing a game, you want to play the game well with everyone around you. True success is when your job is a joy rather than a chore.

The contents of this book thus far came together when I saw a DVD showcasing a phenomenal partnership among 579 volunteers to set a world record in the home building industry. It would shape the next chapter of my life.

BUILDING THE IMPOSSIBLE

I was at the Texas Motor Speedway when I first saw an hour-long DVD showcasing some local area builders. Led by Brian Conaway, they set a new world record by building a 2249-square-foot house from the ground up in under three hours. They poured a concrete slab that dried in only 22 minutes, something that normally takes days to harden.

They timed the building and installation of everything from trim to carpet, light switches to countertops—down to the second. The organization, leadership, motivation and team building was unbelievable. Over 579 volunteers set aside trade differences to form an extraordinary team who built this house.

When the DVD ended, I asked if I could watch it again. As Steve, his father, and I watched the DVD again, I realized that all the leadership principles and core values that I had ever learned were integrated into the story behind this event. I knew then that this could be one of the greatest leadership books ever written.

Brian smiled when I said that, but a week later I met with Steve and Brian again and said, "I want us to write a book about this 2 Hour House experience. I believe this book could impact many lives, maybe move a nation." I still believe this to be true.

Since then, we have created an entire corporation called *2 Hour House* at www.2hourhouse.com. The 2 Hour House epitomizes building the impossible - and the story continues to impact other people, corporations and families as they move out of the world of impossibilities forever. Brian partnered with 579 people to set a world record and achieve the impossible. Now we will begin partnering with thousands of others to build "impossibilities" all over the world.

Nothing defines the purpose of the 2 Hour House better than the paragraph below. This is the new frontier. It is coming to pass even as I write this. Having watched the 2008 Olympics unfold, it is clear that the mindset of breaking rules and breaking records is set to unseat what has been traditionally thought of as 'our limits': "We created a company called Two Hour House, the purpose of which is to teach everyone that "breaking rules, breaking records" is the only game worth playing. There is nothing else in the world worth doing. It's a call to freedom throughout the world. It's a call to the liberation of the entrapped mind, which has always told us we can't do what we dream of doing. Two Hour House says you can. You can transform the world. Let us show you how."

Each House Is Different

The creation process of the Two Hour House company helped me realize why success means different things to each of us. Our homes represent what is most important to us. Younger families may want a two-story home for the extra room, while empty nesters are downsizing as quickly as possible. There may be 20 homes on a city block, but each one has a different layout and different colored walls, carpet, counters and floors. All you have to do is look around the neighborhood to realize that we're different. And yet, we all want peace of mind and success in life and to know that we're making an impact. Peace of mind means different things to different people.

What does an ideal business look like to each one of my employees? Probably not the way I envisage it. It's important to me to ask others what success means to them and understand it from their vantage point. What does success look like from the sales perspective? What denotes success in the tech department? Each area will have a different definition. Whenever I partner with people, I try to remember that we're all unique, and we all want different things.

OPENING DOORS OF OPPORTUNITY

Partnering with other people has opened more doors of opportunity than I could ever have experienced if I'd done things on my own.

During the two years of preparation for the 2 Hour House, Brian shared the vision with hundreds of volunteers who each contributed a part. Imagine hundreds of people looking at the same house from different points of view. An electrician looked at a house and saw something entirely different from what the carpet layer or cabinet installer saw. An engineer would have seen the house from different vantage point than an architect and vice versa.

Sharing his vision resulted in something much greater than he could have accomplished on his own. Reams of paper captured every trade expert's perspective on how to get their part of the project done in the least amount of time possible. When Brian combined all of those perspectives into one master plan, the result was infinitely better than a single viewpoint.

I often ask myself, "What I am currently doing in my life and/or business that is so outrageous that I can only achieve it if I partner with others? How might I be limiting my dreams if I don't share my vision?"

JUST ASK

I wonder what would have happened if I'd never asked the lumber company to come and see the baseball stadium through our eyes. We both saw the vision that day. I might have missed out on a great opportunity to collaborate simply because I didn't ask.

Seven

BEING A LIFELONG LEARNER AND ASKING QUESTIONS

What stops us from asking questions and exploring possibilities? When do we decide it's no longer safe to explore the world around us and adopt the approach of being a lifelong learner? I think it begins when we're young. At some point in our lives, our questions are challenged in a negative way and suddenly we feel diminished. Someone tells us that we should know better, or we're told that we should know it all by now. I'm not sure when "by now" is. It's as if we cross some imaginary line where we think we must either appear to be experts on everything or a fool for having to ask questions.

When we stop asking questions, we start filling in the blanks by assuming what we don't know. When my daughter was in sixth grade, her teacher told the class, **"Don't ask a dumb question."** Well, what is a dumb question? Nobody knew! The students weren't sure if their question met the teacher's criteria for dumb or not - so guess what? No one asked any questions that semester, and I am willing to bet that no one learned very much either. Right there, a whole classroom learned that shutting down was safer.

The only dumb question is the one that we are afraid to ask. No sincere question is dumb. Only by asking questions can we arrive at the destinations we desire.

Socrates was one of the greatest educators. He taught by asking questions. We call it the Socratic method. He drew out the answers from his pupils (which, by the way, is the root meaning of the word "education": *duco*, to draw out). Socrates grilled his students with non-stop questions about specific subjects. He made it safe to learn.

His questions encouraged them to ask more questions to increase their knowledge. What would happen if we implemented this same style of complete, 360-degree thinking today in order to move ourselves and other people toward their goals and not away from them?

It happens to all of us. My wife's story is similar. One day at the beginning of the semester of her ninth grade Algebra class, the teacher (who was also a coach) introduced the class to variables. With a room full of doe-eyed freshmen in their first week of high school, I imagine that the x and y variables in the equations were not the only unknowns that day. These guys and gals had questions - and lots of them. But everyone was too shy to raise their hands and interrupt the big burly man at the front.

Finally, one of the football players ventured a question only to be totally humiliated in front of the entire class. My wife said that from that day forward she never asked the teacher a question for fear of public humiliation.

The truth is that we stop learning when we stop asking questions. And we will never be, do or have to our fullest potential if we don't ask questions that move us toward our goals. The more facts we have about a situation or idea, the closer we are to making wiser decisions.

The alternative is to pretend we know something that we don't. Instead of being motivated to find out the answers, we learn to fake it, to stay safe. Instead of being lifelong learners, we cheat ourselves out of the opportunity to truly know instead of assuming, and assuming can be a very dangerous thing.

Just Readin' It *Ain't* Gettin' It

Several years ago, I was speaking to a large group of financial advisors. I love asking questions. I asked this group of successful men and women, "How many of you have read Steven Covey's book, *The Seven Habits of*

Highly Effective People?" About half the people in the room eagerly raised their hands. Then I asked, "How many of you can recite all seven habits?" Not a single person could.

We can read material without internalizing it. We love it, we agree with it - but we don't really know it. For example, we can't practice the habits of effective people if we haven't internalized them.

It's like telling a good joke. When I hear a joke, I have to practice it several times before I can tell it easily enough to make others laugh. It's the same way with learning. If I haven't internalized it, I just know I'll never practice it.

There is an old proverb that says, "What we don't know can't hurt us." Wrong! What you don't know *can* hurt you. I heard about a man who rushed into a pharmacy and said to the pharmacist, "Quick! I need something to stop the hiccups!" The man rushed down an aisle in the store looking for a product to help.

As he was searching the shelves, the pharmacist snuck up behind him and hit him with a karate chop to the neck and hollered, "Boo!" The stricken man looked up from the floor, rubbed his neck and said, "What in the world did you do that for?"

The pharmacist smiled and said, "Well, I'll bet you don't have the hiccups anymore." The man said, "I never did! It's my wife out in the car who has the hiccups!" What we don't know *can* hurt us!

As a business owner, I can assume that I know the best way to handle a dispute among employees without asking a single question. How much more effective would my resolution be if I took the time to ask enough questions and identify the real problem? When we don't ask questions, we start to fill in the blanks from a limited source of knowledge and make assumptions that may be totally incorrect and, worse, harmful.

What could have been a weakness in our family system has instead become a great strength. I am not afraid to ask questions or to admit when I don't know something. I'm always quick to say, "I know that I don't know!" When I became the guardian of my brothers and sister, I didn't pretend that I automatically knew what to do. I read a lot and asked a lot. I found people more than ready to help me with challenges I encountered along the way. I just had to ask. Learning to ask is like having gold nuggets in your pocket.

MENTORING 101

I believe mentoring is the fastest way to advance in any area of life - our work, our faith, our health. Mentoring is primarily a relationship between students and teachers. As we grow, we learn that when the student is ready the teacher will appear.

Mentoring Thrives On Curiosity

When a child is old enough to talk, one of their favorite words is, "Why? They ask, "Why is the sky blue? Why is the grass green?" Children are naturally curious about how the world works, and parents are natural mentors to them.

Our kids can drive us crazy sometimes with the "why's" of life, but every question presents us with a teachable moment. Saying, "I'm glad you asked" reinforces their willingness to learn to know what they don't know. We have to train children to ask questions to speed up and enhance their mental growth.

Another lesson I learned in a parenting class called *Growing Kids God's Way* is that when a small child tears a plant from the ground, a parent's first reaction is to say; "No, don't touch that." The child's first reaction is to say, "But why?" This parenting class taught me to say, "No, don't touch that because if everyone grabbed flowers, there would be no flowers in the world." It's just looking at it a different way and honoring the question they asked.

Somewhere along the way we stop asking those childlike "why" questions. When we allow someone to mentor us, we have to reawaken that natural curiosity about life. Our independent, do-it-yourself culture may be losing the art of mentoring because we're too scared to ask for help and advice. We also experience fewer opportunities to mentor others because no one's asking us any questions either! We're all guilty of contributing to an epidemic of ignorance and stagnation.

Look Who You're Asking!

Why is it that we ask people in the same boat as us for advice? Many successful people are more then willing to share their ideas with others. Once their cups are full, they have more to share and they want to share it. It's lonely at the top!

Find the person who seems to be, do and have more of whatever it is that you want in life and start asking questions. With any of my goals, I have always looked for a mentor whether the goal is financial, social, spiritual or physical. If I want to lose weight, I would ask someone who has succeeded in a healthy diet and weight loss program. If I wanted to pursue a new business venture, I would ask a successful business person. It's a whole lot easier to follow a path that somebody else has already traveled.

We often don't tap into a source of success that's staring us in the face - our family. They tend to be valuable advisors. They understand our background and can gear their advice to fit us better. If we think we only inherit our physical genetics, we're sadly mistaken. One of the things I wish we did more of as a society is to learn from each other, generation to generation. We need to take the time to interview our mothers and fathers and grandparents to determine the important lessons they have learned about life, relationships, business and success. One would think that we should improve from one generation to the next, but we tend to repeat ineffective patterns because we don't ask and so we don't learn.

Ask Mentors Specific Questions

I've never stopped having mentors, and I still ask as many questions as I need to achieve my goals. In fact, I recently called a gentleman at the largest financial planning firm in Canada. He is sixty-seven years old and a master at acquisitions in an area similar to the one I want to master. I didn't know him, but I told him what I was trying to do and said, "I'd like to learn from somebody who's been there." I asked my favorite two questions: "Do you believe that anybody can learn from their mistakes, but a smart person learns from other people's mistakes? And do you believe that when the student is ready, the teacher appears?" He laughed, but the next thing I knew he was on a plane flying to Texas to meet with me.

He graciously shared many of the things he'd discovered along the way, including valuable lessons he learned from his mistakes. He helped to clarify the do's and don'ts. If I'd pursued the acquisition phase of business on my own, I would have probably made some costly mistakes trying to figure out what he already knew to avoid. His insights equipped me with the confidence I needed to proceed with my own endeavors. Once he'd agreed to meet with me, I took the time to write down my goals and detail exactly what I wanted this success to look like. If you are able to let a potential mentor know exactly what you are trying to accomplish, they will often be glad to help you attain your goals.

I asked him everything. *"What makes you tick? What lessons did you learn along the way?"* Think of the first question you ask someone when you pick them up at the airport. You ask, "How was your trip?" When you see someone who has already arrived at a place in their life journey where you want to be, ask them, "How was your trip?" If you want to be the best at something, find someone who is already excelling in it and ask how they did it.

Have Several Mentors To Gain
Different Perspectives

Having mentors in several areas of our lives allows us to grow faster than doing it on our own. Different aspects of life require different mentors. Yet the overriding principle is the same. If we are prepared to learn, our mentors can give us wings. Like good books, each of them contains a gem waiting to be uncovered. They also overlap. The person we think of as a business mentor may very well turn out to offer us some of the wisest life lessons to be had. Good mentors are wise shortcuts. Reinventing the wheel has no merits, standing on the shoulders of another makes giants of both participants.

It works the same way with books. One good book may introduce you to two or three others that all contribute different perspectives on the same topic.

QUESTIONS WE RARELY ASK

Have you heard the proverb, "To be understood, you must first seek to understand?" For me, to be a lifelong learner and keep asking others questions, I have to make sure that I listen attentively. Thanks to my brother John, I have learned to listen to people, with my mouth shut and my ears and eyes open. People are drawn to sharing with someone who values what they have to say. Being a good communicator often means being absolutely quiet. Stillness speaks.

On the other hand, people shut down when they come across as know-it-alls or fix-its. They have nothing to add and so they withdraw. Assuming we know everything about someone else or their situation without asking any questions says, "I don't care enough to let you tell me." I see couples and families in my office who have never discussed their feelings about important issues, but you can sure see the frustration and hurt in their responses.

"Why Is That Important To You?"

I once knew a man whose sole motivation for his financial strategies was to create more security for himself and for his family. It was very important to him because he didn't have any sense of financial security growing up. His wife, on the other hand, came from just the opposite experience (a different paradigm). She grew up in a wealthy family where financial security was never an issue—it was a given. Her philosophy was, "Everything is going to be okay no matter how much you spend."

This gap in their understanding proved to be a major obstacle in their relationship. She would scold her husband because he was always questioning every financial move they made. If she bought something expensive, it would drive her crazy that he would worry about if they really could afford it (which they could). Likewise, he could not understand why an issue that was so important to him seemed irrelevant to her. They talked about money constantly, but they never asked each other what that one little word meant to either of them.

When this couple went through the process of discovering their unique personal values and what was most important to them about money, they realized their core issue was linked to how they were raised. She finally understood for the first time why he was asking all the questions that caused conflict in the marriage. While he realized how his wife's family influenced her thinking about money.

Once they began to ask each other questions about what was important to each of them, they were both more open to the other's perspective now that they understood the "why" behind their actions. It changed their marriage. She no longer feels threatened by the questions. And he doesn't resent her spending money. They learned that loving each other meant that he needed to understand what was important to her, just as she needed to understand his feelings about the need for security.

All too often we hold ourselves back when we don't ask for what we want from others, and we don't seek to understand their perspective. We create a whole library of false beliefs, resentments and unnecessary concerns from bad information (or the lack of it).

"Do You Understand What I Need From You?"

Anytime there is a breakdown in communications at home or at work, we have to start asking questions. It's easy to misunderstand the facts when you don't ask questions. That's usually the case when something doesn't get done or something goes wrong.

When I'm part of a communication breakdown, the first thing I do is ask myself if I've clearly communicated my expectations. In fact, when I present information to a group or individual I always ask for feedback. I want to know if they understand what I want. I may not have clearly communicated what I was thinking at the time. Or, the listeners may have internalized the information a different way. To get that clear stream of communication flowing, I can't assume anything. Asking someone, "Do you understand?" is not as effective as asking someone to put in their own words what they hear you saying.

"Why Do You Ask?"

When I was a young man starting out in business, whenever someone asked me my opinion, I blurted it out without thinking. For instance, if someone asked me my opinion about a certain football coach, I'd tell them exactly what I thought. More often than not, I ended up sticking my foot in my mouth because I just insulted their favorite team! One day a good friend of mine told me, "Whenever someone asks you for your personal opinion, you should say 'Why do you ask?' so that you won't get your foot stuck in your mouth!"

That one piece of advice has helped me immensely because that small sentence draws a mine-full of information and places the question straight back in the hands of the original questioner. More information and facts equip you to make wiser decisions. If I say, "Why do you ask?" That person might tell me he or she is a raving fan of that team and I'll know what not to say! By saying, "Why do you ask?" I understand the motives behind their question.

"Why Not?"

As I look at everything I have or do not yet have in my life in terms of success, I often ask myself one important question: *Why not?* Why aren't I doing what I dreamed I'd be doing by now? Robert F. Kennedy once said in a speech:

"There are those that look at things the way they are, and ask,' Why?' I dream of things that never were, and ask 'Why not?' The future does not belong to those who are content with today, apathetic toward common problems and their fellow man alike, timid and fearful in the face of bold projects and new ideas. Rather, it will belong to those who can blend passion, reason and courage in a personal commitment to the great enterprises and ideals of American society."

CHAPTER Eight

NEVER TAKING LIFE'S GIFTS FOR GRANTED

By the time I was nineteen, I had worked my way to the top sales position in appliances at Montgomery Wards. I felt like I was king of the world. Although many of the people I worked with were twice my age, customer service came more naturally to me than most. I also had a great command of brand names from dishwashers to electric stoves. My family's financial security was assured.

Or so I thought.

Turns out, reaching that level of success and responsibility at such a young age wasn't the best thing that could have happened. However, what I learned as a result of sleeping in a little late here and there turned out to be a valuable life lesson.

The star salesman, I started showing up for work after everyone else had clocked in for the day. I was a college student burning the candle at both ends trying to earn money and take a load of credits. I knew I should be on time, but I told myself, "I am the number one sales guy. What are they going to say to me?" Soon, my one-hour lunch stretched into an hour and a half. I would come in, ready to hit the floor and make some sales, yet I was still half an hour later than everyone else on the team. "There is no way they are going to let *me* go," I kept telling myself. "They need me, so what difference does 30 minutes make?" I soon found out.

They fired me.

I was absolutely shocked. I couldn't afford to be without a job, so I went to my professor in engineering (I was majoring in petroleum engineering at the time) and asked him if anybody in the oil business was hiring. He told me to contact two of his friends in off-shore drilling down in New Orleans, several hours away. After a long, lonely drive to New Orleans (only to find out they weren't hiring), I was in a quandary.

I was working to help support my younger siblings and help my mom. As I drove back home to Texas, I was desperate and down to my last twenty dollars. Somewhere around Beaumont with several hundred miles to go, I made a phone call. It was one of the most difficult conversations I've ever had, but one that changed my future.

I called my former boss.

The quarters stuck to my sweaty hand as I deposited them into the payphone and dialed the store. While they transferred me to my supervisor's desk, I took a deep breath and considered what I would say.

"Hello?" The woman's voice came on the line.

"Hi, it's José," I said in my most upbeat voice. Long silence. "Do you believe in learning from mistakes?" I asked. There was an even longer silence.

Fortunately, my supervisor eventually said that yes, she did believe in learning from mistakes. I promised her that if she let me have my old job back, I'd be on time and I'd never take advantage of the situation again. Would she consider talking to me?

By the time I hung up, I had an appointment with her on Monday morning. However, this was Friday, and as I rolled back into the parking lot of my apartment complex, I knew another difficult conversation lay ahead because I had no money left to pay my rent.

I walked into the rental office to speak with the landlord. A few minutes later, I left the rental office and went straight to my apartment. I put on an old t-shirt and jeans, walked outside to the maintenance garage and pulled out a red push lawnmower with a greasy handle. It took some convincing, but the landlord agreed to accept my rent later that month if I mowed the lawn and did some odd jobs around the complex over the weekend.

Not surprisingly, I had to work in another department when I returned to Montgomery Wards on Monday. It hurt me that I couldn't go back to the appliance department that I knew so well. However, my whole attitude had changed. Before I lost my job, I took advantage of my position. The company couldn't do without me. Now, I knew differently.

APPROACH LIFE AS A GIFT

I guess we all fail to appreciate all that we have until the moment we're in danger of losing it. What's most important in life we tend to take for granted—from our relationships, to our jobs, to our homes. We get so busy making a living that we forget how precious life is.

Karl Wallenda, the patriarch of the tightrope act The Great Wallendas, once said, "Being on the tightrope is living. Everything else is waiting." Once you experience what you know in your heart is "really living," it becomes impossible to take another moment for granted.

You can imagine, of course, that Karl Wallenda never waltzed in late to a tightrope performance. He never slacked off or gave what he was doing half his attention. He couldn't afford to. This immigrant circus performer knew that life was a precious gift because he was in danger of losing it every day. He had the privilege of living (and, ironically, dying) doing what he loved every day. If you're not doing whatever that is, you've neither found your place, nor fully realized that life is a gift.

Appreciate Today

Part of the problem is that we spend so much of today waiting for tomorrow. When it's winter, we can't wait for spring to arrive. After a few months of spring and summer, all we can think about is when it will cool off. We wait for someone's call, we wait for our next raise, and we long for our next vacation. Meanwhile, life is busy happening all around us.

When we are so focused on waiting for tomorrow to get here, we begin to take for granted all that we have today. Having a passion for possibility means we're constantly thinking about and planning for the future. At the same time, we're firmly rooted in today.

Let's take business as an example. Some companies start looking for new business all the time when they need to be taking care of their current clients. Your existing clients are the lifeblood of your business, not the new group you want to attract. If you take care of people they will take care of you, too.

In my business, we constantly focus on appreciating what we have now and enhancing those relationships.

I have an expanded definition of client. I look at my employees and my vendors as clients as well. If I take the time to nurture all of these relationships today with the same special care and attention I would give to a client, tomorrow will take care of itself.

Jimmy Durante once quipped, "Be nice to people on your way up because you meet them on your way down." When you believe that anything is possible in your future, you see people differently. Every relationship gains that much more significance. Think about the young college student at the front desk of your gym. Let's say that every time you see him you strike up a conversation and ask him how it's going at school. You treat him with kindness and respect. It's possible that 15 years later he could be the next HR manager for a huge company that wants to do business with you. All because this young man remembers how you treated him.

When I teach young people at Junior Achievement I often ask them, "Do you know someone who loaned you five dollars that you didn't repay?" Or maybe you loaned someone five dollars and they didn't pay you back? The kids usually look around and laugh nervously because they've all been there. I say, "Do you realize that if you don't pay someone back, you're making a statement about who you are 20 years from now?"

Now that I have their attention, I tell them, "That person who loaned you money that you didn't pay back? That person will grow up and know not to do business with you because you showed them what kind of person you are."

Everything you do today affects tomorrow. When you learn to appreciate everything and everyone in your life, you open yourself up to potential blessings down the road. Relationships are exponential and far reaching. Each has the potential for positive results in the future. You never know where one act of kindness or generosity will lead.

NOT TAKING RELATIONSHIPS FOR GRANTED

Once people get out of college, they don't stay in touch. It's as if they can walk away from friendships, but I never could do that. I've made a concerted effort to stay reasonably connected with 90% of the friendships I had 20-30 years ago.

When I graduated from college, I knew everybody would start drifting apart once they had their own families and kids. I wanted to create an event where my fraternity brothers and their wives and families would come back together to celebrate each year. There wasn't much to do in Tyler in those days, so two days before New Year's Eve the year after graduation, everyone pitched in five dollars to throw together the first of many annual New Year's parties.

Because I chose to stay in Tyler and build my family and business in this community, I was developing new relationships, too. Soon this little fraternity brother party grew into a Tyler New Year's celebration event that included hundreds of people! Every year for 20 years, people came from all over to dress up, dance and create New Year's Eve memories. In later years, we even had to rent a community hall when 800 people showed up one year all dressed in formal wear. It was incredible.

One of the best things about the party was the fact that everyone paid their own way (especially when hundreds of people were involved). I've never believed that anyone fully appreciates a free lunch when they would rather do their part. The best parties are not necessarily the high-dollar affairs where everything is catered. Some of the most memorable get-togethers occur when everyone contributes. That annual event taught me about not taking life for granted. It was a time to appreciate all of the relationships God had given to us and celebrate that together.

Priorities Change

Of course, priorities change. After 19 years of this annual tradition, my daughter came to us two weeks before the party and asked, "Mom and Dad, when can I spend New Year's with you?" She was ten years old at the time. My wife smiled and said, "When you're 21, you can come," (knowing that a ten-year-old would not have much fun at a formal dance for adults). My daughter looked hurt and said, "You mean I have to wait 11 more years to celebrate New Year's with my parents?"

I realized she was right.

I told my family that we were not going to have the party next year and that we would be together as a family from now on for New Year's Eve. The next year, we were celebrating at the stroke of midnight somewhere in the ocean under the stars on a cruise.

I still value the friendships with those from my fraternity. Now I host family functions that include all of their families as well as mine. I simply had to find a way to value my expanded circle of friends, and I still don't take any of them for granted.

APPRECIATING LIFE MEANS BEING TEACHABLE

When I was coaching little league, one of my best players was a fifteen-year-old with the worst work habits I'd ever seen. At practice, I would catch him slacking off in the outfield relaxing on one knee. The kid was talented - more talented than any of his peers because he had matured faster. I could tell by the look on his face that he was thinking - *What's the point?*

Inevitably, the other kids would notice and they too would begin to slack off. Not only did I have a responsibility to help this player get over his laziness, I felt like the whole team was suffering as a result.

I did something radical. I benched my best player for the next three games. When one person breaks the rules and falls short of the expectations, it affects everyone else. Team morale happens anywhere you find groups of people working together, whether it is a church, a business, a family or a junior league.

The boy's father came to me all upset about my decision to bench his son. I stood my ground and told him that it was going to be the best lesson for him. If I let him shrug off his responsibility to the team, even though he was good, it would just reinforce lazy work habits that would follow him all his life. "He'll be done forever," I tried telling the angry father (who also happened to be a friend and client). He wasn't convinced and walked off in disagreement.

If this weren't a true story, I'd say that the kid shaped up for the next game, rallied his teammates, apologized profusely and was a different kid from that day forward. However, things didn't happen that way.

He quit.

After riding the bench for the third time, my best player walked. I wanted to teach him and the other kids on the team that we had to treat practice like a game situation because life doesn't give us practice tries. It's the real thing.

He eventually called me up, apologized and told me he would change his attitude. In fact, he went further than anyone else in the league. Today, he still thanks me for the splinters in his behind that he got riding that bench for all those games.

College scouts don't necessarily look at what you do on game day. They want to see your work ethic in practice. They want to know one thing; no matter how good you may be or how talented you are: *Are you coachable?* They would rather have a coachable person than somebody who thinks he or she knows it all because an attitude like that will damage the team culture.

People get comfortable just getting by. They may be at the top of their game for awhile, but taking that position for granted always leads to negative results.

ASSUMPTION IS THE ENEMY OF APPRECIATION

When I became the legal guardian of my younger siblings, they were in high school. Early on, I sat down with them at the kitchen table at our mom's house and asked them point blank what they expected of me. We had to be a little more grown up in those days than most people our same age, so they took this conversation seriously.

They started giving me a list that included things like paying the rent for Mom, making sure they were taken care of and providing food on the table. As a college student working and going to school full time, I explained to them that if I didn't work and follow my obligations, I would lose the family home. I showed them how bills worked and the ins and outs of running a household.

Next, I asked them what I should expect from them. They suggested doing their part around the house, getting good grades, picking up after themselves, respecting Mom, going to bed on time - all the things that they could control.

I wrote the two lists in two separate columns on a legal pad. I'll never forget that once we looked over that little piece of notebook paper, we all three signed it as if it were a legal document. It was a huge lesson for them and a significant turning point for me in the value of clear communication. Everyone clearly understood their role in the future success of our family. No one assumed what the others would do. This way, we would guard against taking each other for granted. However, one of the greatest challenges I had as the new head of my family dealt with this very issue.

When my younger sister was seventeen years old, she worked in my office answering the phone and doing odd jobs. As her guardian and head of the family, I paid for family expenses like the insurance on her car. Typical of a high school student, she didn't take her job working for big brother seriously. She was chronically late and would go to her cubicle in front of the other employees thirty or forty-five minutes past the hour.

I called her into my office one day and told her if she was late one more time I would have to let her go. That meant no more gas money. No more paying for insurance premiums. Nothing.

A few days later, she was late again. I will never forget the look of shock on her face when I told her to pack up her desk and go home.

I cut off her insurance and gas money and didn't give her a dime from that day forward. It was the hardest thing I ever had to do.

I think she expected me to come around in a few days when I saw how she was struggling. However, after a month, she knew I was serious. She applied at a fast food restaurant nearby and started working there. Would you believe that this teenager who couldn't be on time anywhere soon became employee of the month?

Later, she found a better-paying job at an equipment company and was a model employee. She was up at seven in the morning and was never late. Years later when she came back to work with us at the firm, she was a different person.

Assumption is the enemy of appreciation. We don't appreciate what we assume will always be there. People often don't appreciate the job they have until they lose it and have to start looking for work. They often don't appreciate good health until something goes wrong.

The moment we start making assumptions about the permanency of a relationship, or a job, or our health we begin to devalue it. Loss sometimes acts as the jolt we needed to stir us from our assumptions.

LIFE'S BEST GIFTS OFTEN COME IN DISGUISE

Sometimes I forget that my negative experiences contain gifts.

What I think of as the worst experiences in my life, turn out to be the best thing that could have happened.

I coached my little brother Jeff's Senior League baseball team when he was about fifteen years old. There was a play at the plate and amid a huge cloud of dust the umpire stepped forward and barked at my player, "You're oooouttt!" Only the player was actually safe.

During the next inning, Jeff was warming up on the pitcher's mound when he overheard the home base umpire admitting to the second base umpire, "Man, I blew it on that last call."

I was standing back in the dugout watching Jeff when suddenly he began using sign language to tell me exactly what the umpires were saying! No one else knew what Jeff was doing. I made my way onto the field and up to the home base umpire.

"So you know you threw the call, huh?" I said to him. I'll never forget the look on his face.

Seeing that umpire hem and haw was worth every minute of growing up with deaf parents. I wish I had a nickel for every time that I'd resented having to speak sign language as a young kid. You don't always feel appreciative of everything that happens in life especially when you're convinced you've gotten a raw deal. (Of course, that umpire never admitted he threw the call—he threw me out of the game instead! But I smiled all the way back to the bench.)

When you react to life's challenges with negativity, what can you expect to happen other than more disappointment and negative outcomes?

LOOK FOR MOMENTS TO CELEBRATE

When you look at life from a positive perspective, you will always find something to celebrate, and celebration is the fuel that keeps us going. We need to acknowledge every milestone along the way. Every time I finish what I've set out to do, I take time to appreciate the step fully *before* eyeing the next goal.

CHAPTER | *Nine*

RECOGNIZING THE GOOD IN EVERY PART OF LIFE

I go walking at night with my daughter - something we've done since she was six. She once told my brother when he asked about her favorite things to do with her dad that she loves those walks. We like to go at the end of the day just as everyone is winding down for the night. We leave our cell phones behind so no one can interrupt "our time". For the first 100 yards or so, we just take in the silence of the evening. Pretty soon, we strike up a conversation about what's happening in our lives. Sometimes I throw out a quote from a book that I'm reading, or one I've heard on a tape, and she tells me what she thinks of it. We always finish our walk with a question that has become a tradition, "What two things are you proud of today?" It takes more thoughtfulness to think about the good things that happened in our day than to simply blurt out the bad stuff, which doesn't make us feel good anyway.

One of the things I am proud of everyday is my family. Popular culture suggests that busy fathers and their daughters can't be close. I've read sad statistics about how many fathers only spend an average of seven minutes a day talking to and interacting with their children. Apparently, teens and parents aren't supposed to get along. Current thinking implies that being estranged from our kids when they're teens is normal.

It's as inaccurate as saying, "Every boss is difficult." Or, "After twenty years of marriage, you can't expect to be in love anymore." Or, "Older parents are a burden on their children." I figured out a long time ago that these statements are frequently excuses for not working at our relationships.

While I don't expect things of people, I expect myself to find the best in people. I look for the good in every person I love as if I were looking for treasure, and I celebrate all that I find.

DO WE FORGET TO CELEBRATE THE 'STATUS QUO'?

It seems to me that as we move forward in our lives, we forget to celebrate the steps got us there, and we even forget to celebrate each key point of arrival. Thanks to a few bumps in the road that scared the heck out of me, I found a jewel in life that I love to celebrate. It's that beautiful word called "normal." When I look at many other people's "normal", I am reminded every day to be grateful for my own. What we consider "poor" in this country would represent wealth in other countries. For example, most homes have a TV, a microwave, a dishwasher, a car, DVD player, computer and cable television, along with fast food a couple times a week. That is unheard of in a large number of countries around the world, like Africa, China, Central America and India.

The next thing that I've learned to celebrate humbly and gratefully is my own achievements. When you begin to understand your full potential and look at what you are doing every day in actually fulfilling it, being the best version of yourself takes on a whole new meaning. It's a lesson in humility or a kick in the pants. I never forget whose hand is at my back. I never forget to say thank you. I never forget to celebrate.

It's a way of honoring the source of the lessons and gifts received. Celebration is simply out loud appreciation.

I am still learning that it is okay to want to be, do and have more in life. We are taught from the time we are small not to be greedy. That's like telling a kid in the candy store, "Don't touch and don't taste!" The opposite is important. The more we envision for ourselves, the likelier we are to do good things around us, simply as a byproduct of reaching for our own dreams. Aspiration breeds imagination and leads to innovation.

I once helped a colleague of mine put some of her future goals down on paper so she could begin mapping out some realistic steps to get there. Her dream included a certain standard of living and driving a certain type of car. Later, she shared her list with a friend who made the off-handed comment that her list seemed "greedy." This hurt my colleague immensely and she began to question the validity of her goals.

We have to learn to live without worrying about what other people think. There is a sense of freedom when you begin to celebrate life on your own terms. You can either live in heaven or hell in your own mind. You can be miserable trying to live up the standards of others. Or just be and do the best that you can and experience a little bit of heaven on earth.

We limit ourselves when we let others tell us what and when to celebrate. And sometimes we are our own worst enemy.

Sometimes Life Is About Losing And Then Winning

If one of the keys to being, doing and having more in life is celebrating all the good things in our lives, then we have to be able to secure our anchor in those good things even when we experience trouble or disappointment. Sometimes there are hidden gems in losing, if we know where to look for them.

My little league team had a perfect record season after season.

No one scored a touchdown against us. These kids were proud of their perfect record. Then a team from Dallas came to town. These guys were the biggest grade school kids I had ever seen in my life, and they mowed my little guys down like weeds within the first five minutes of the game. It's difficult to deal with losing when you're used to winning all the time. We had a roster full of skinny, scrappy and scrawny. But we were the smartest team by far. I'd always reminded them, "Smart beats strong."

I stood there clenching my jaw as they limped over to the sidelines. They unsnapped their helmets and before I knew it I had 11 little boys all bawling on the bench. I drew a deep breath and said, "Boys, we all knew that this would be a challenge. We're stepping into the big leagues, and we have to expect a few bruises along the way. I am proud of us because we are tackling something bigger than ourselves. Part of winning is growing and being challenged." With that, I clapped my hands, slapped some shoulder pads and sent them onto the field. Our opponents scored on us again in the next series of play.

We ended up with our first loss in three years, but none of us were defeated. We'd all just taken on a giant for the first time, so we were elated. This happened two weeks before they would enter junior high.

I knew how tough it was already going to be on these kids without the added challenge of having their self-confidence on the line. Only now they knew they could handle giants and challenges.

The parents were more frustrated than the kids, who "got it." The kids and I ate pizza and celebrated stepping up to the challenge. Many of those kids played on both the T.K. Gorman High School and John Tyler High School Championship teams as seniors.

I'm convinced my guys learned something more valuable than a win on the scoreboard. They learned that sometimes winning all your games is not as important as how you view the loss.

Finding something good in every situation means being open to what you can learn through difficulty. If you're teachable, even the tough times will work in your favor. Winston Churchill, who triumphed over the Nazi regime in WWII, had some good advice about overcoming adversity. He said, "If you're going through hell, keep going."

Don't Rsvp To A Pity Party

When we face trials, it is tempting to throw a pity party in honor of what's going wrong in our lives rather than to recognize all that's going well. I like this anonymous rhyme about pity parties:

I had a little party

this afternoon at three

T'was very small, three guests in all

just I, myself and me

Myself ate up the candy

and I drank up the tea

Twas also me who ate the cake

And passed the pie to me

You may receive an invitation to a pity party in your honor, but don't RSVP!

One thing we have in our family is a lot of love. It doesn't matter how much money someone has or doesn't have. Sure, there were times when we were tempted to feel depressed or feel sorry for ourselves. But that never lasted for long.

Together, we made it through when we had to scramble to come up with fifty dollars in rent money. We made it through when the air was blowing through the walls of our home because the nucleus in each of these experiences was the love we have for each other. And you just can't put a price tag on that. Instead of feeling sorry about the tough times we've been through, we look back and see all of the good things that happened all around us despite it all. And that's worth celebrating. Albert Einstein wisely said, "There are only two ways to live your life. One is as though nothing is a miracle. The other is as though everything is a miracle."

Oh, The Places We've Been!

One of the exercises I like our office to do at the start of a new year is to write down everything we accomplished last year so that we can reflect on a job well done. Goal-setting is crucial because it creates measurable milestones for success.

Showing what a business or a family has accomplished together is a treasure map. It shows all the places we've been and where we're headed next. Sometimes we look ahead to next year forgetting to credit the year that's past for all the lessons and the gifts. You may not be, do or have all that you want just yet—but make special note of what you've accomplished in your life thus far, and head for the future with the fuel of past success driving you forward. A family or business that regularly takes time to celebrate their accomplishments and the impact they had on others is more likely to stay successful.

Do you ever get the feeling that you're not moving forward fast enough? You can gain a better sense of how far you've come when you take the time to celebrate milestones on your journey to success. It will also help you determine which direction to take next.

Being Part Of Something Grand

Is the vision you have created for your life worth celebrating? Is it something so outrageous that if and when it happens you will feel like throwing a huge party? Think back with me to the story of the 2 Hour House. What inspired those people to dedicate several years of their lives to something that everyone was telling them couldn't be done? They wanted to be part of something grand. People want to be part of something special.

People in a family, a business or a team get excited once they understand that the direction you're taking will allow them to be part of something that's much bigger than them. It's like being invited to be part of the magic. Our book, *2 Hour House*, shares a story about one of the volunteers who felt like he was part of something extraordinary.

I'll never forget a story Dick Schilhab told about one of the concrete truck drivers who later moved to another town. The manager from a trucking company in the new town called Dick one day as a routine check on the guy's references. In the course of the conversation, the manager let Dick know an interesting thing about his application.

On it, the driver had written, "I drove for the *2 Hour House*." Tell that guy that his job that day (although brief in the big scheme of things) wasn't important. His sense of pride and ownership during the event was a result of raising the expectations for everyone who participated. For him to say he drove for the 2 Hour House meant something to that man beyond filling in blanks on an application.1

Celebrating being part of something grand creates a culture where people feel connected to something larger than themselves. When we start identifying all the ways we are making a difference in the world, we create cause for celebration, and then even the smallest things we do take on new meaning. Albert Giacometti, a sculptor, came to this realization when he said, "Basically, I no longer work for anything but the sensation I have while working." That's finding true joy in your work and life - no hidden agendas, no manipulating others. No thought of, "What's in it for me?" Just pure exhilaration.

Little Things Mean A Lot

As the guardian for my siblings, I understood the importance of attending their school and sporting events. I wanted to make sure that they always knew someone cared enough to celebrate and support their goals.

One time, I drove two-and-a-half hours one way just to watch my sister's five-minute swim race just because I wanted Juanita to know that I was there to support her. I only missed one of my brother Jeff's games in his whole high school basketball and baseball career. We still talk about it because he hit the final shot and won the game. It was on the front page of the sports section of the local newspaper. Just my luck!

CELEBRATE OTHERS

One of the greatest gifts we can give to someone else is encouragement when they're too tired or busy to see anything noteworthy in themselves or their situation. Sometimes, we just need to let them look through our eyes and see themselves from a different perspective.

I have a Character First card that I always carry in my wallet. At our company Christmas party one year, I listed every employee in our firm and associated each one with a particular character trait I saw at work in their lives. I thought about words like *honorable, hospitable, dependable and trustworthy.*

When I came to flexibility, I named two or three people and explained how I saw that trait at work in their lives. I came to the word, *forgiving* and I named two or three others.

I noticed that even when it was not somebody's turn to be honored, each person was looking around, smiling at each other and nodding. It was as if they were acknowledging, "Yes, I see that trait at work in that person, too." Suddenly we all realized we were part of a very special group of people - people who were sincere and unusually thoughtful and tolerant and responsible.

Talk about cause for celebration - the atmosphere in that room lit up with the sense of pride we felt toward one another. It made us all realize that we have the best people on the planet working together toward something significant. Who wouldn't want to be part of something like that?

THRIVE ON ENCOURAGEMENT

My mother is the greatest example of finding the good in every situation. In my family, I'm surrounded by people who are positive thinkers and who are open to all kinds of possibilities.

If you have big dreams and big goals ahead of you, do yourself a favor. Seek out others with the same philosophy and approach to life.

I call them, the people who motivate. Be on the look out for similar souls who share your belief that everything is possible.

CHAPTER Ten

SURROUNDING YOURSELF WITH PEOPLE WHO MOTIVATE

I'm always thinking about tomorrow. When someone is on the Moon, I'm already at Mars.

As a father, I remember my daughter wobbling down the hallway toward me when she was just learning to walk. As she took those first steps, I was already thinking about what life would be like when she was a teenager. I was so afraid it would all go by too fast. I remember saying to myself that in just 10 short years this little grinning child, stutter-stepping her way down the hall toward my open arms would be saying to me, hands on hips, "Dad, you just don't understand!"

In fact, much to my wife's chagrin, I took out a video recorder when my daughter was small and recorded a message for her to listen to in anticipation of that day. I told her in that message that I knew the time was coming when she would be a teenager and would feel like Dad no longer understood her or her world. Even so, I would always love her and be there for her.

Sure enough, the years flew by as predicted. Recently, we had a situation where she wanted to do something and I said no. Would you believe the words that came out of her mouth? "Dad, you don't understand! Get with the times, Dad, so and so is doing this . . ." The timing was perfect. I grinned at her and asked her to wait while I went and got that 10 year old tape. I sat her down and we watched it together. Nothing more needed to be said.

You don't have to have a teenager at home to realize that life is moving us forward at a rapid pace. Racecar driver, Mario Andretti, observed, "If everything seems like it's under control, you're just not going fast enough." Some people prefer a snail's pace and are content to languish in past achievements and accomplishments. I never get tired of the thrill of hugging the curves and shifting into the next gear toward the future. I like being around people who fuel your enthusiasm for your dreams.

KNOWING ANYTHING IS POSSIBLE

Some people know exactly where they want to go and how to get there. Most people have little idea. Few of us have been taught to dream or expect more. Many of us allow life's current to carry us along without giving much thought to where it is taking us. Ben Franklin once said of this type of attitude, "Blessed is he who expects nothing, for he shall receive it."

Many of us don't think we deserve much. Convinced we don't deserve the dream, we invent excuses and let our dreams die a little every time we utter a logical disclaimer.

Positivity attracts good things even during the so called tough times. I don't like to settle for less. That's what passion for possibility is all about. I have learned to surround myself with people who feel the same way. The people who will motivate you will have certain characteristics, beginning with a clear vision.

People With A Clear Vision

Alan Kay, a pioneering computer scientist and one of the leading players in the computer revolution has said, "The best way to predict the future is to invent it." You must surround yourself by people who have a clear vision of a definite future and who are willing to work toward it - even if they have to "invent" it.

Alice learned this lesson in Alice in Wonderland when she was searching for a way out of Wonderland and came to a fork in the road. "Would you tell me, please, which way I ought to go from here?" she asked the wise Cheshire Cat. "That depends a good deal on where you want to get to," the cat responded. However, Alice replied that she really did not much care. The smiling cat told her, "Then it doesn't matter which way you go."

Having a clear vision of a bright future comes naturally for some people. They are progressive thinkers. They are insatiably curious. They are obsessed with how things could be, rather than how they are. Other people are more comfortable living in the past and only have a clear recollection of how things "used to be." The majority of us, shockingly enough, are *taught* to expect less.

A clear vision allows you to see the blue sky of a sunny future - even if it's raining today. By contrast, some peer at a bleak future from a dark-clouded perspective; possibility-thinking scares and frustrates them. Looking for people who have the ability to communicate this vision to others in a way that makes sense and inspires, will allow you to work faster and more effectively toward your common ideals.

People Who Think Positively

Another characteristic of the people who will motivate you is unapologetic and continual positive thinking. I think Henry Ford was right when he observed, "Whether you think that you can, or that you can't, you are usually right." Similarly, people with positive attitudes and outlooks on life can affect a group for good. Their upbeat personality and optimism is infectious. You want that kind of attitude replicating itself and spreading throughout the group.

People Who Want More

Once you have achieved what other people said was impossible, it liberates the entrapped mind that tells us that dreams are things that can't be done. That adrenalin-pumping experience of succeeding where you were afraid you might fail makes you want to do it again. It is addictive.

Sadly, most people settle for less than their best and for less than life's best. Good leaders avoid people who limit themselves and gravitate towards, and surround themselves with people who want more out of life.

After everyone in my office read the 2 Hour House book, people started policing themselves more about how they approached problems and challenges. I didn't have to tell them that nothing was too hard or too difficult to overcome—they began to believe it for themselves. Over time, it evolved into knowing it. Once people are familiar with living life on a higher level, they realize that is the only game worth playing. When possibility-thinking takes over an office or a team and you begin to do what others thought was impossible, the culture changes. It's charged with newfound excitement and enthusiasm for what's next. Walt Disney said it simply, "It's kind of fun to do the impossible."

PEOPLE WHO SUPPORT YOU

I once went with the Tyler Jaycee's to a legislative seminar in our state capital, Austin. They hosted a mock legislature where we would try to adopt and push through bills dealing with a variety of topics.

As one of the representatives, I had six bills to push through. The first bill was on term limits, and even though I was a little nervous, I volunteered to go first. When I began presenting my bill, three other men on the opposite side of the floor stood up to counter my proposal. As I had learned to do in our instruction time before we got started, I yielded the floor to them. They began chopping up my bill like an Iron Chef!

Suddenly, I realized I had made a tremendous mistake in yielding the floor to them so soon. Not surprisingly, my bill fell short by two votes. And it was my easiest bill of the session with five to go!

As I was sitting there devastated, three more seasoned representatives introduced themselves to me, the obvious rookie. One of the bigger men said, "Never yield to the opposition. What you need to do before your next bill is to pick five or six people who agree with you. Stack them up on the other side of the room and have them throw softball questions to you and see if you can hit them out of the park."

(By the way has anybody notice that this has become the norm for politics these days).

With my supporters firmly seated around the room, the effect was much more positive, and the next five bills sailed through with ease. Mahatma Gandhi, in his fight for the independence of India, said of the opposition, "First they ignore you, then they laugh at you, then they fight you, then you win."

Inspiring leaders always build a supportive environment by outweighing the opposition with their enthusiasm. When you have an idea, piggyback off other supporters passion for the concept as it's being introduced - don't try to carry it off all by yourself. You can affect an entire room with a positive attitude toward a new idea if you've gathered enough people beforehand to express their support and enthusiasm.

People Who Believe In You

When my brother Jeff was in the fourth grade he really loved his teacher. He came home with straight A's and couldn't wait to go to school each day. I hadn't seen his face light up about school that way before, so I was curious. It turned out, the teacher was tapping into Jeff's enthusiasm by communicating to him that she believed he had great potential. She motivated him, encouraged him and gave him a lot of self-confidence as a student.

In the same way, we increase our potential and productivity exponentially when we feel like someone believes in us. Their confidence in our ability boosts our own self-confidence and encourages us to persist through difficult times. Of course few of us realize that our potential and productivity increase the most when we invest in the priceless gift of believing in ourselves.

People Who Want To Grow

Surrounding yourself with highly motivated people who want to keep growing is hard because they are rare. I actively seek out people like that.

Someone who is eager to learn and grow through challenge is inspiring to everyone around them. When you are around those who thrive on personal challenge, you will no longer be satisfied with your own status quo.

In professional bicycle racing, the best teams learn to work more effectively by practicing a strategy called "drafting." Cyclists will often race in tight-knits packs to reduce drag and the amount of energy it takes to maintain their speed. Applying this principle in the context of groups, it's easier for like-minded individuals to accomplish great things together because of the cumulative positive effect they have on each other.

Creating Your Own Flow

Big dreams show you what's important to you in your life. Conforming to popular 'can't be done' opinion, is like wearing a sweater several sizes too small—it doesn't fit right and it limits your freedom.

There will always be negative people who tell you that you can't achieve your goals for one reason or another. Very few people still believe that anything can happen. I like to be around those people.

The more I align myself with others who think positively about the challenges ahead, the less resistance I encounter as I move in the positive flow of energy they create, and the faster I can move forward with my dreams and goals.

People who are happy

There's a popular saying, "If Momma ain't happy, ain't nobody happy." That's true in many circumstances. Everyone pays when an unhappy person is in a position of influence. I learned this when I joined a law suit abuse organization in the early nineties. Our motto was, "We all pay. We all lose." This referred to lawsuits where a jury awards exorbitant amounts of money in damages to offended individuals over something frivolous. What many people don't realize is that an insurance company doesn't pay the claim. The business or firm does not pay the claim. We all pitch in and pay the claim through increased premiums. One unhappy person's complaint has the potential to affect us all.

I've discovered that wealthy people aren't necessarily happy people. Some of the most miserable people on earth have all the money in the world. Have you ever noticed how often unhappy people travel in packs? The law of attraction exists and it works. If you live a life that exhibits happiness, you will attract other people who are happy. If you focus on negative thoughts, you'll attract others with similarly negative thoughts.

People who are happy have learned to control their fears and attitudes in such a way that nothing is able to steal their inner joy. These are the kind of people who motivate you, even when things look bleak.

IS IT EVER TOO LATE FOR YOUR DREAM?

Traditionally we have always accepted that we can wait too long to start being, doing and having all that we want in life. As if there is a time limit on it. You may have heard some people divide life into three time periods: the go-go years (20s-60s), the slow-go years (60s-70s) and the no-go years (70+).

Those imaginary lines lock us in and lock up our dream capacity. We say to ourselves, "Oops, missed that deadline! Time to give up and pack those dreams away." Some people will try to pigeon-hole you in the slow-go or, worse yet, the no-go years when it seems that life is more precarious. In the last while, I have begun to understand that these limitations might very well prevent some of the finest ideas in life from becoming a reality.

I always say to enjoy the journey so that you don't look back and say, "I wish I would have done . . ." Live life to its fullest now - whatever your age. Adult children often tell their parents, "Go enjoy your money and live your life." Still, most people hold back and they don't live the quality of life that they really want.

In my experience, many people who are *there* financially and even have *excess* money - are not doing the things they really want to do in life. In the greater scheme of life, there are more important things than money. Life begins when you can recognize that. Albert Einstein once said, "Not everything that can be counted, counts, and not everything that counts can be counted."

Luxury is being able to focus on what counts. Remember those dreams you packed away? Kids really mean it when they say they want you to go and enjoy life. It gives them peace of mind when they know you're having a ball.

We could all benefit from re-learning to think like a child and live for the moment. The past is the past, and the best we can do with it is learn from it and then leave it respectfully where it belongs. We have a choice regarding what we want to do from this day forward. Life is about living in the moment and consciously making choices that will affect our future for the better.

YOUR PASSION FOR POSSIBILITY

A few days after I gave my marathon speech about Your 26 Miles to that graduating finance class, I received a note in the mail from one of the students. At the end of my speech, I had recommended three books for those who wanted to learn more about pursuing goals and getting more out of life.

This student said he had already read all three books and asked me if there was anything else he could read in a similar vein. With graduation around the corner, most students were taking a break from books at that point and selling them back to the campus bookstore as quickly as they could. However, here was a student who had a passion for possibility. It takes a highly motivated person to do what this student did.

As I folded the note into my desk drawer, I thought, "That's the kind of person I like to surround myself with." I called the university, found his number and talked with him about his future plans. Within the next month, this young man, a new graduate, became a valuable member of our firm's team.

I'm still amazed at all the puzzle pieces that clicked together to get me to where I am today. When I graduated from high school and threw my hat up into the air, I had little idea what I was going to do with the rest of my life. As that hat hit the ground, my main thought was that I was out of high school forever. I knew I was going to go to college, but I did not know what major I would have or exactly what I wanted to study.

Nevertheless, I remember reveling in the fact that a world of possibilities lay open before me. I felt sure that I could be anything I wanted to be, do whatever I dreamed of doing and have anything that hard work and desire could bring.

Then reality hit.

My first job after graduation was flagging with a road construction company for 13 hours a day in the Texas heat, earning $4 an hour. This was not my dream job. With the sun beating down on my brow and beads of sweat stinging my eyes, it didn't take long for the value of continuing my education to sink in. I realized that the hot Texas sun was sapping my dreams, and my world of possibilities was shrinking. That's when I started setting goals. My first goal was to save enough money all summer to be able to have my own apartment, buy some used furniture and begin classes at the local junior college in the fall.

Twenty-two years later, I am more aware than ever that life is a marathon. I may have grown up since those high school days, but I still have the fiery belief inside that the whole world is open to me. I have achieved many of my life's goals so far, but in some ways I feel that I've barely begun!

Marathon runners will tell you that running is a way of life. Similarly winning is a habit. There is always another race to run. While you are chasing one dream, the next one is lining up. A competitive marathon runner may run several races in a year. While they are training for the Boston marathon, they may already have their eye on the

New York marathon.

Running a marathon is not an end in itself. It's just one goal that leads to another one. In your lifetime, you will run several marathons depending on the nature and scope of your life's goals. As soon as you complete one, you ought to have another one in your sights.

Truly lucky people live their lives on purpose and are passionate about possibilities. They never stop growing, stretching and reaching. They have goals for their job, their marriage, their children, their finances, their retirement, their community service, their personal growth - even their golf handicap!

When you're ready to face what's next on your list, be prepared to encounter a whole new set of possibilities and options. Change may be uncomfortable, intimidating and even downright scary. Don't be surprised if the wind picks up and you have to quicken your steps. Remember this: you are entering the race that you were born to run.

PASSION *for* POSSIBILITIES

"When we set our dreams in writing, reality Begins"

NOTES

Passion *for* Possibilities

"When we set our dreams in writing, reality Begins"

Notes

_____

_____

_____

_____

_____

_____

_____

_____

_____

_____

_____

_____

_____

_____

_____

_____

Passion *for* Possibilities

"When we set our dreams in writing, reality Begins"

Notes

Passion *for* Possibilities

"When we set our dreams in writing, reality Begins"

Notes
